FAR OUT
FOLKTALES

STONE ARCH BOOKS
a capstone imprint

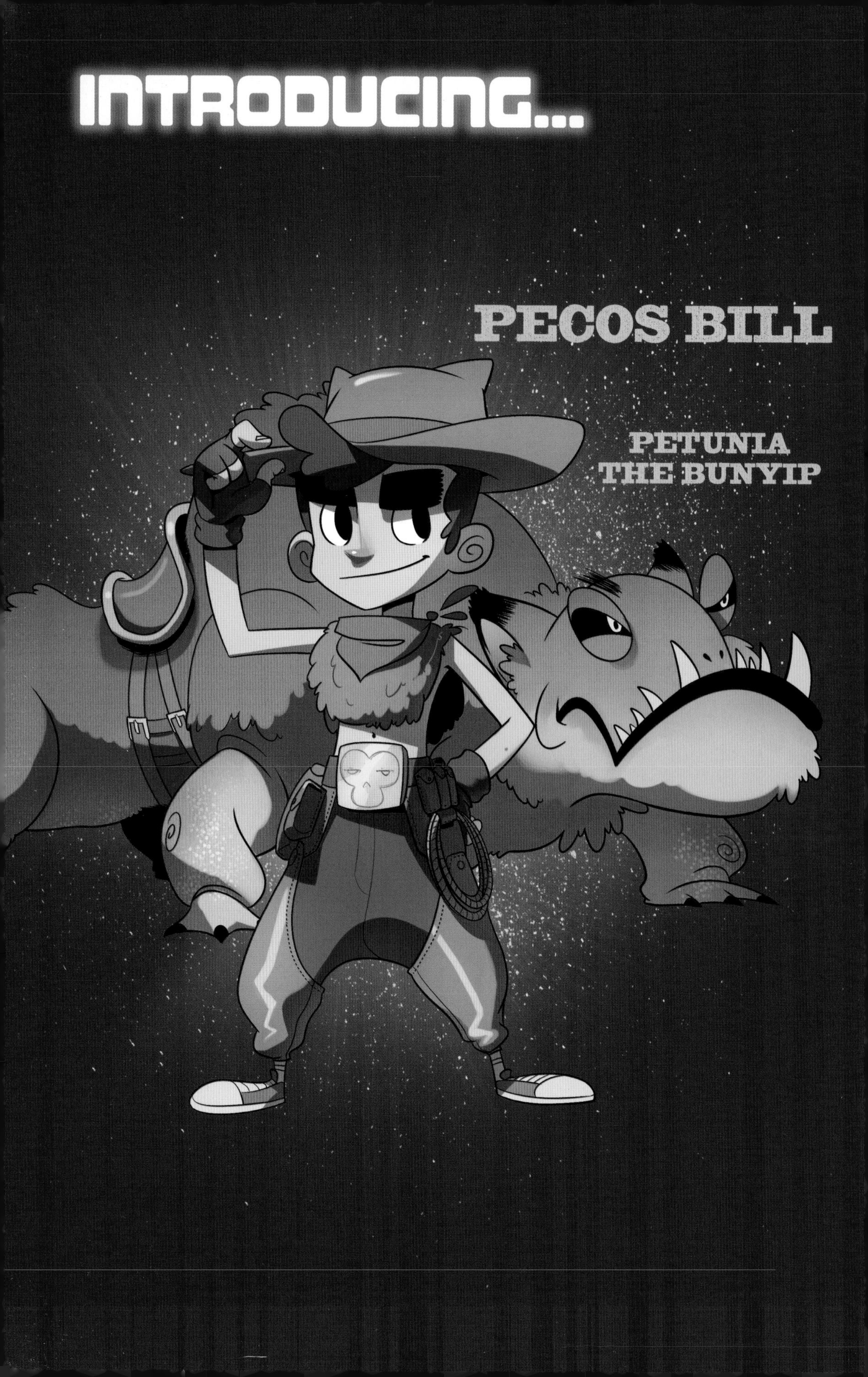
INTRODUCING...
PECOS BILL
PETUNIA
THE BUNYIP

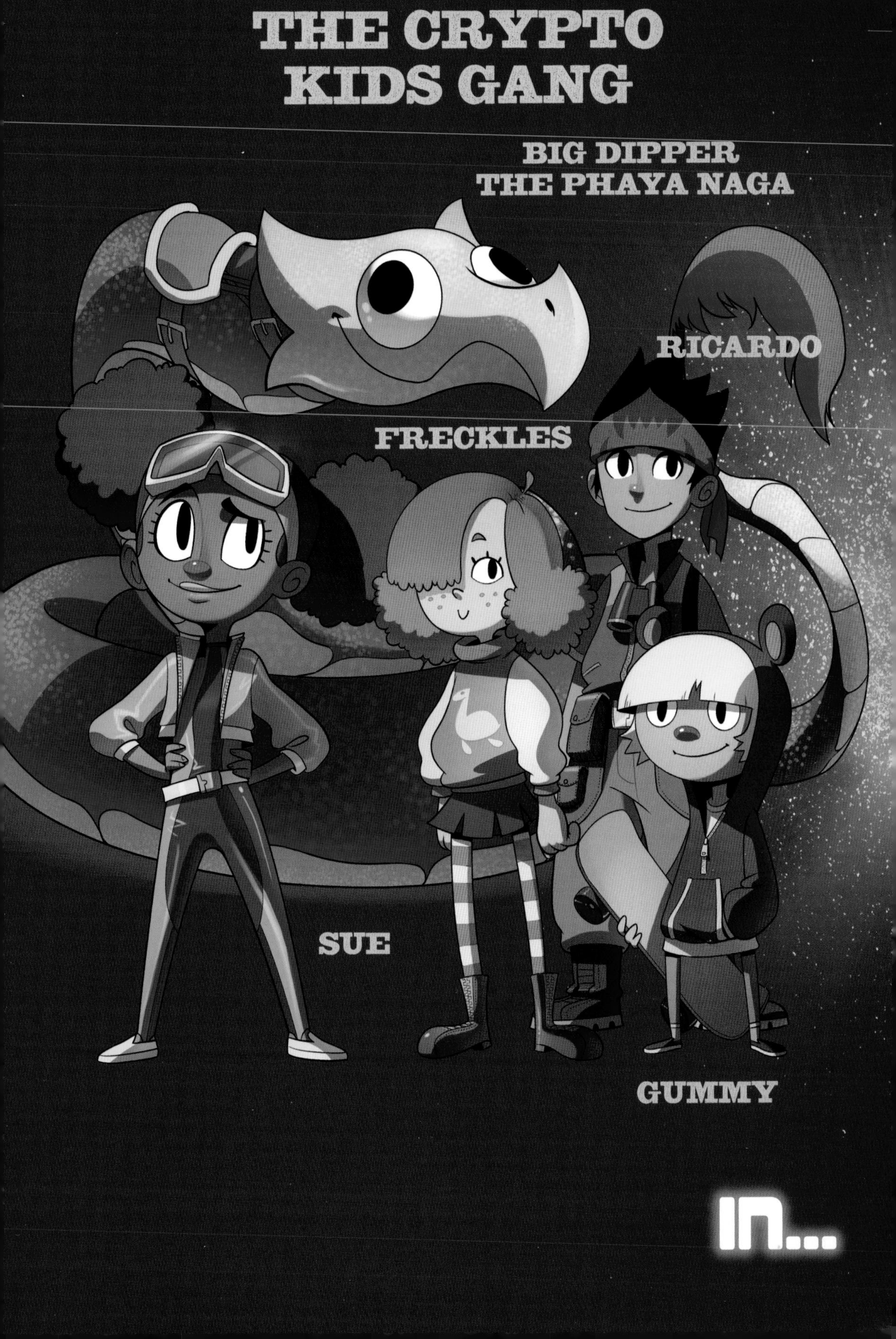
THE CRYPTO KIDS GANG
BIG DIPPER THE PHAYA NAGA
RICARDO
FRECKLES
SUE
GUMMY
IN...

Far Out Folktales is published by
Stone Arch Books
A Capstone Imprint
1710 Roe Crest Drive
North Mankato, Minnesota 56003
www.mycapstone.com

Cataloging-in-Publication Data is
available at the Library of Congress
website.
ISBN 978-1-4965-7841-9 (hardcover)
ISBN 978-1-4965-8006-1 (paperback)
ISBN 978-1-4965-7846-4 (eBook PDF)

Summary: Raised by Sasquatches, Pecos
Bill can tame any critter—whether it's a
chupacabra or the Loch Ness monster.
But when he joins the Crypto Kids Gang
to share his skills, he faces a bucketload
of trouble. Their ranch is getting
crowded, a tornado is heading straight
for them, and a girl named Sue wants to
ride Bill's bunyip. Are some challenges too
monstrous for even Pecos Bill to rein in?

Designed by Brann Garvey
Edited by Abby Huff
Lettered by Jaymes Reed

Printed and bound in China.
966

FAR OUT FOLKTALES

PECOS BILL, MONSTER WRANGLER

A GRAPHIC NOVEL

by **Benjamin Harper**
illustrated by **Fern Cano**

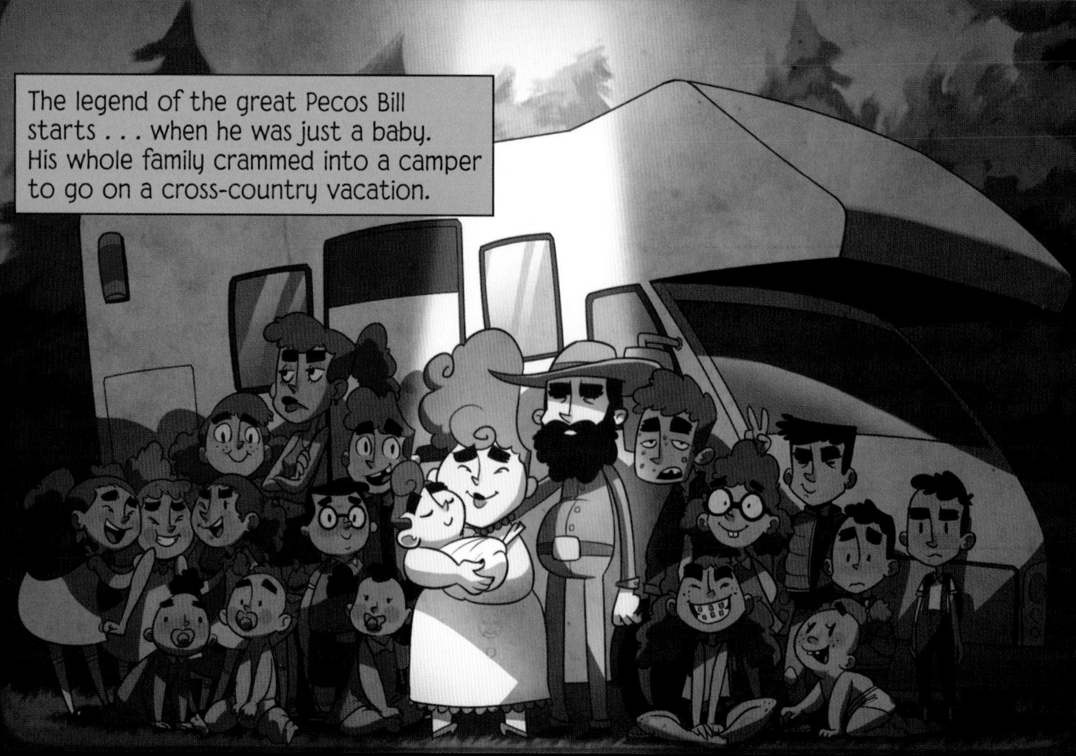
The legend of the great Pecos Bill starts . . . when he was just a baby. His whole family crammed into a camper to go on a cross-country vacation.

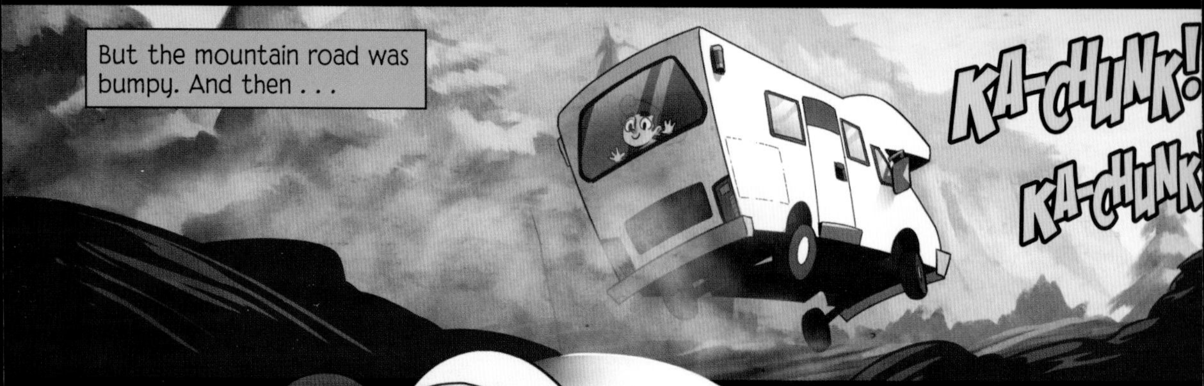
But the mountain road was bumpy. And then . . .
KA-CHUNK!
KA-CHUNK!

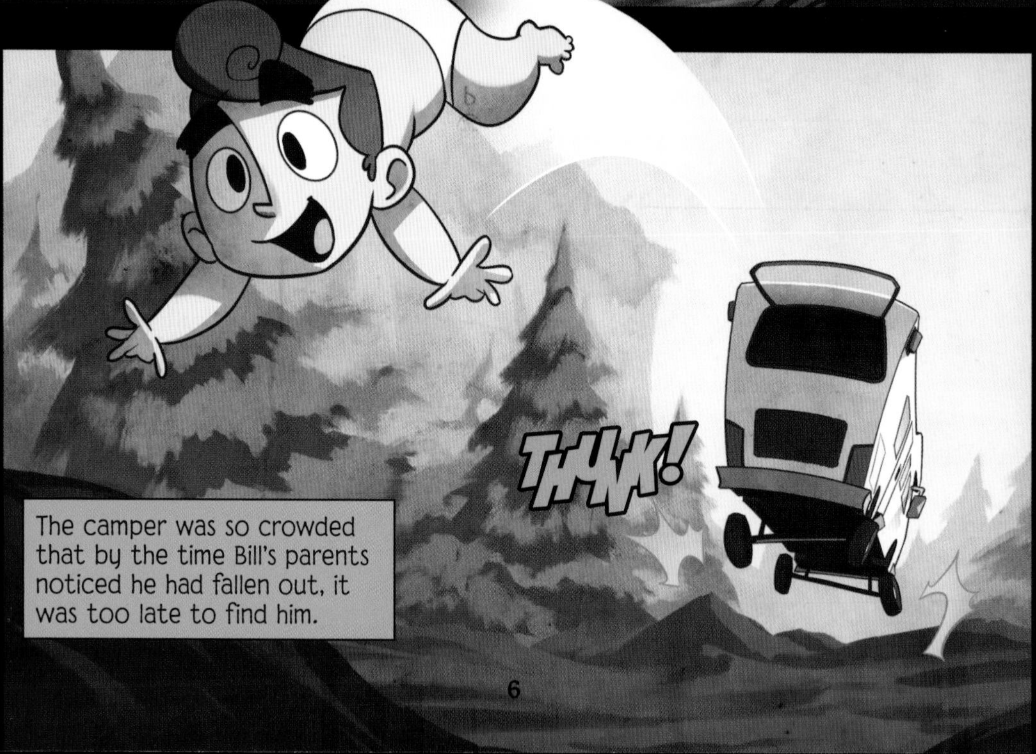
THUNK!
The camper was so crowded that by the time Bill's parents noticed he had fallen out, it was too late to find him.

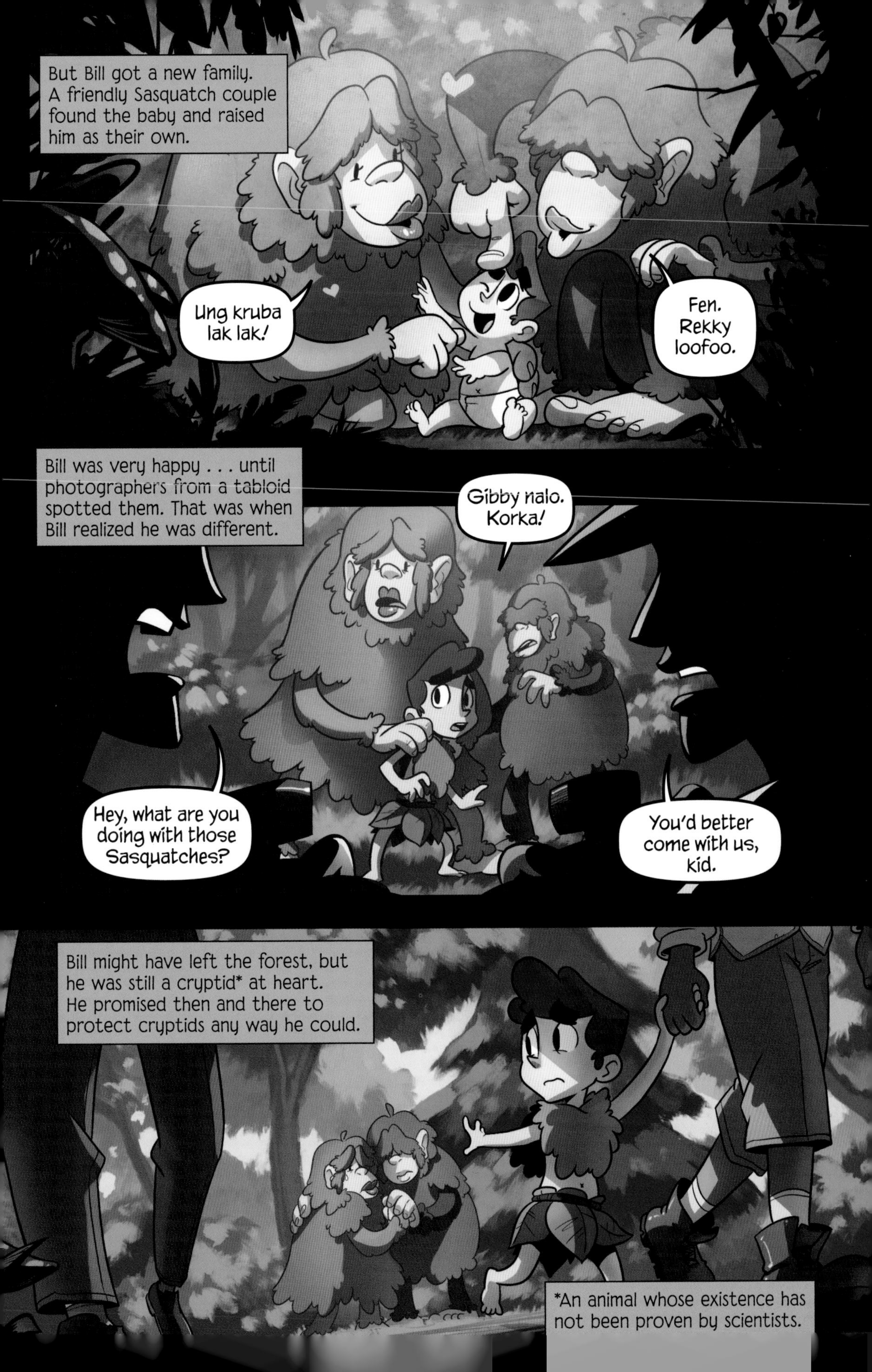
But Bill got a new family. A friendly Sasquatch couple found the baby and raised him as their own.
Ung kruba lak lak!
Fen. Rekky loofoo.
Bill was very happy . . . until photographers from a tabloid spotted them. That was when Bill realized he was different.
Gibby nalo. Korka!
Hey, what are you doing with those Sasquatches?
You'd better come with us, kid.
Bill might have left the forest, but he was still a cryptid* at heart. He promised then and there to protect cryptids any way he could.
*An animal whose existence has not been proven by scientists.

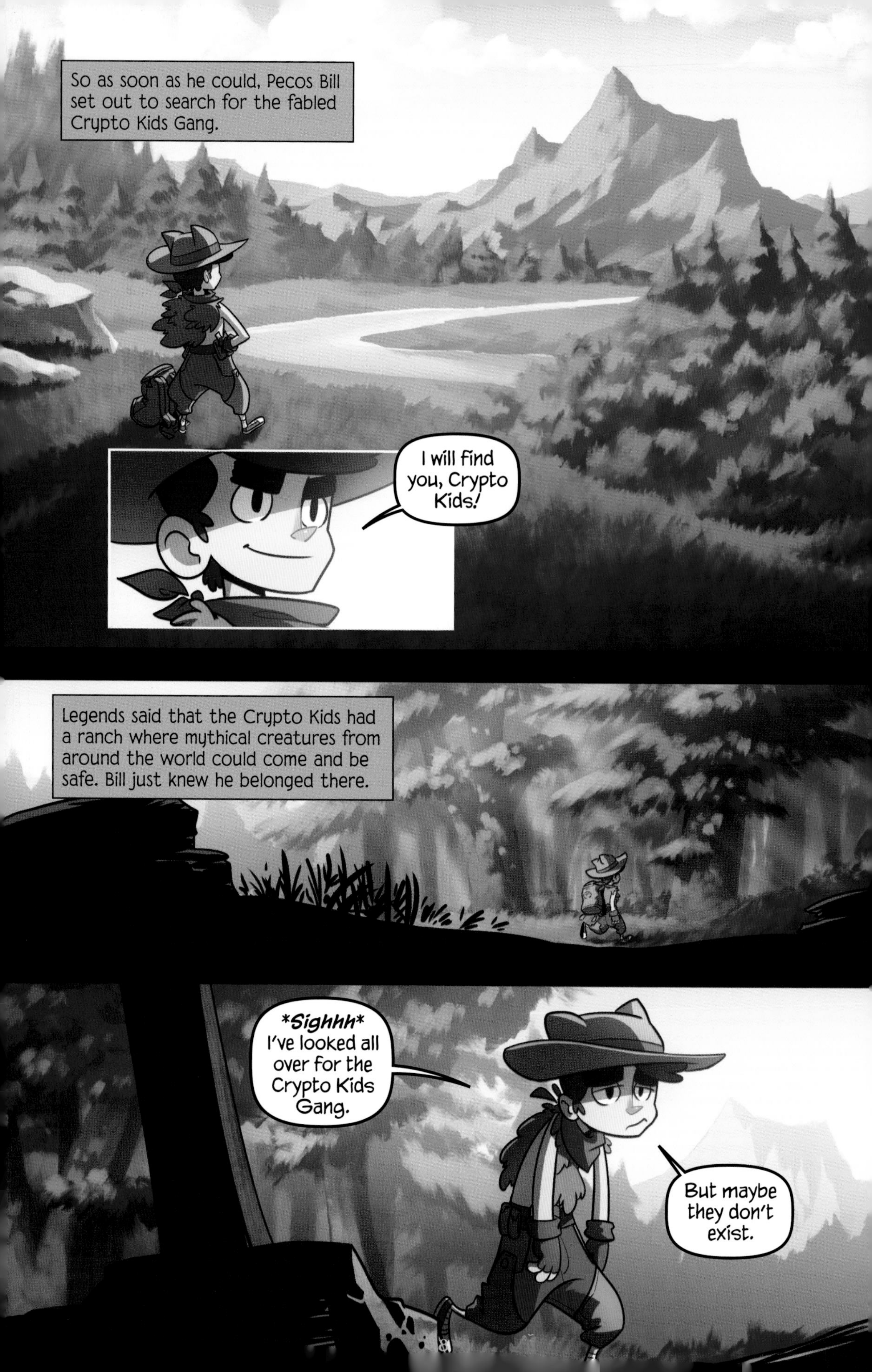
So as soon as he could, Pecos Bill set out to search for the fabled Crypto Kids Gang.
I will find you, Crypto Kids!
Legends said that the Crypto Kids had a ranch where mythical creatures from around the world could come and be safe. Bill just knew he belonged there.
Sighhh I've looked all over for the Crypto Kids Gang.
But maybe they don't exist.

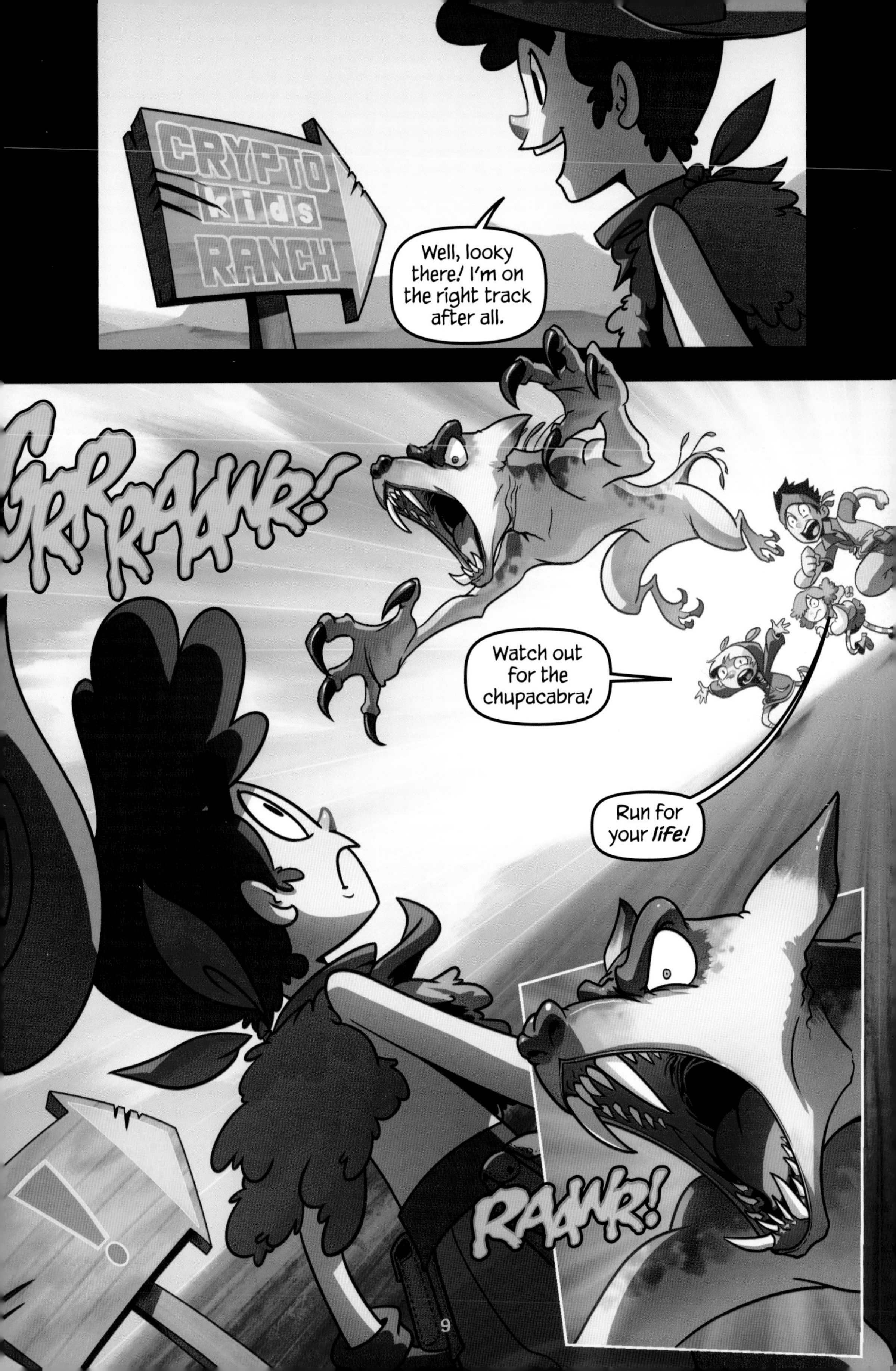
CRYPTO kids RANCH
Well, looky there! I'm on the right track after all.
GRRRAAWR!
Watch out for the chupacabra!
Run for your *life!*
!
RAAWR!

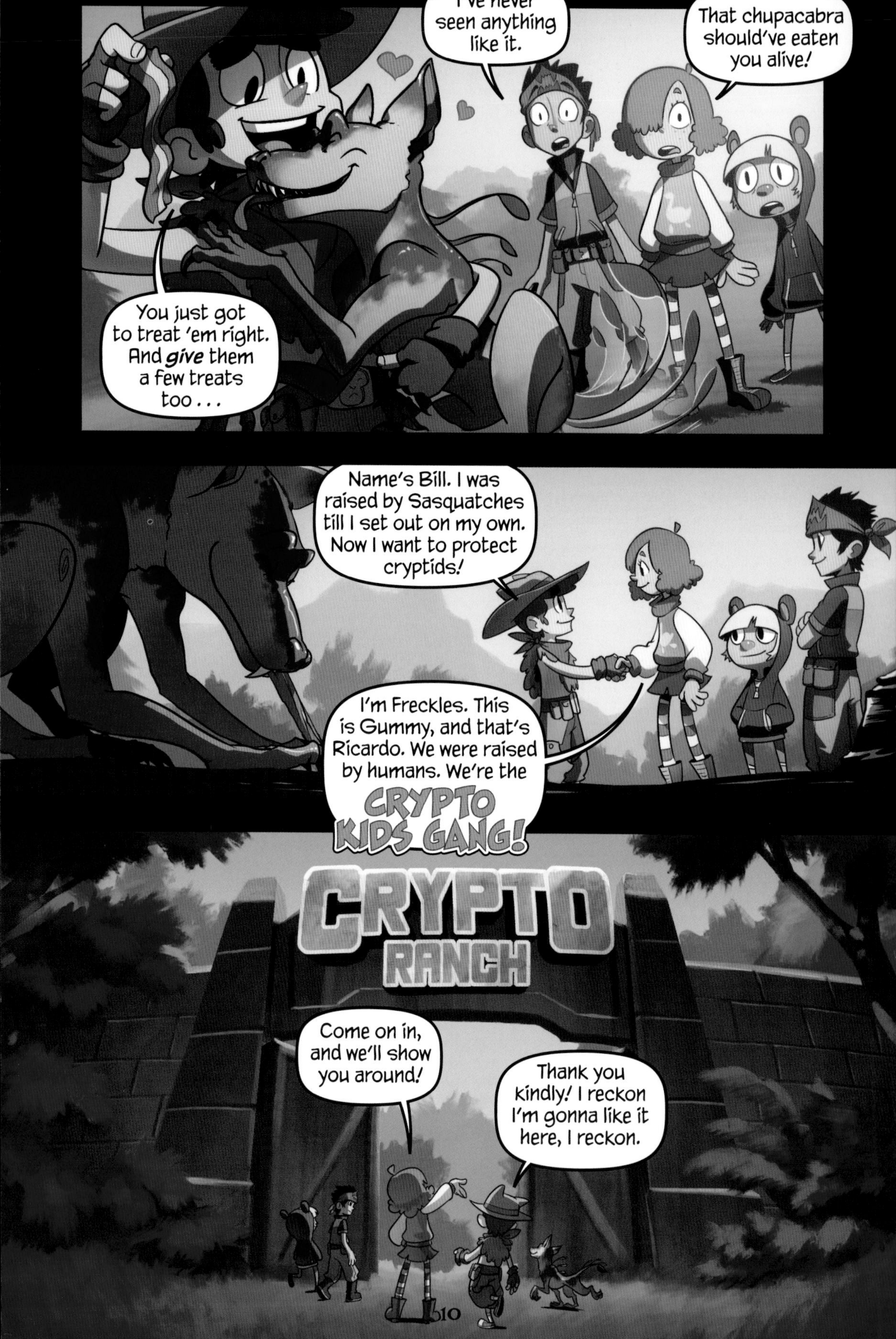

I've never seen anything like it.
That chupacabra should've eaten you alive!
You just got to treat 'em right. And *give* them a few treats too . . .
Name's Bill. I was raised by Sasquatches till I set out on my own. Now I want to protect cryptids!
I'm Freckles. This is Gummy, and that's Ricardo. We were raised by humans. We're the CRYPTO KIDS GANG!
CRYPTO RANCH
Come on in, and we'll show you around!
Thank you kindly! I reckon I'm gonna like it here, I reckon.

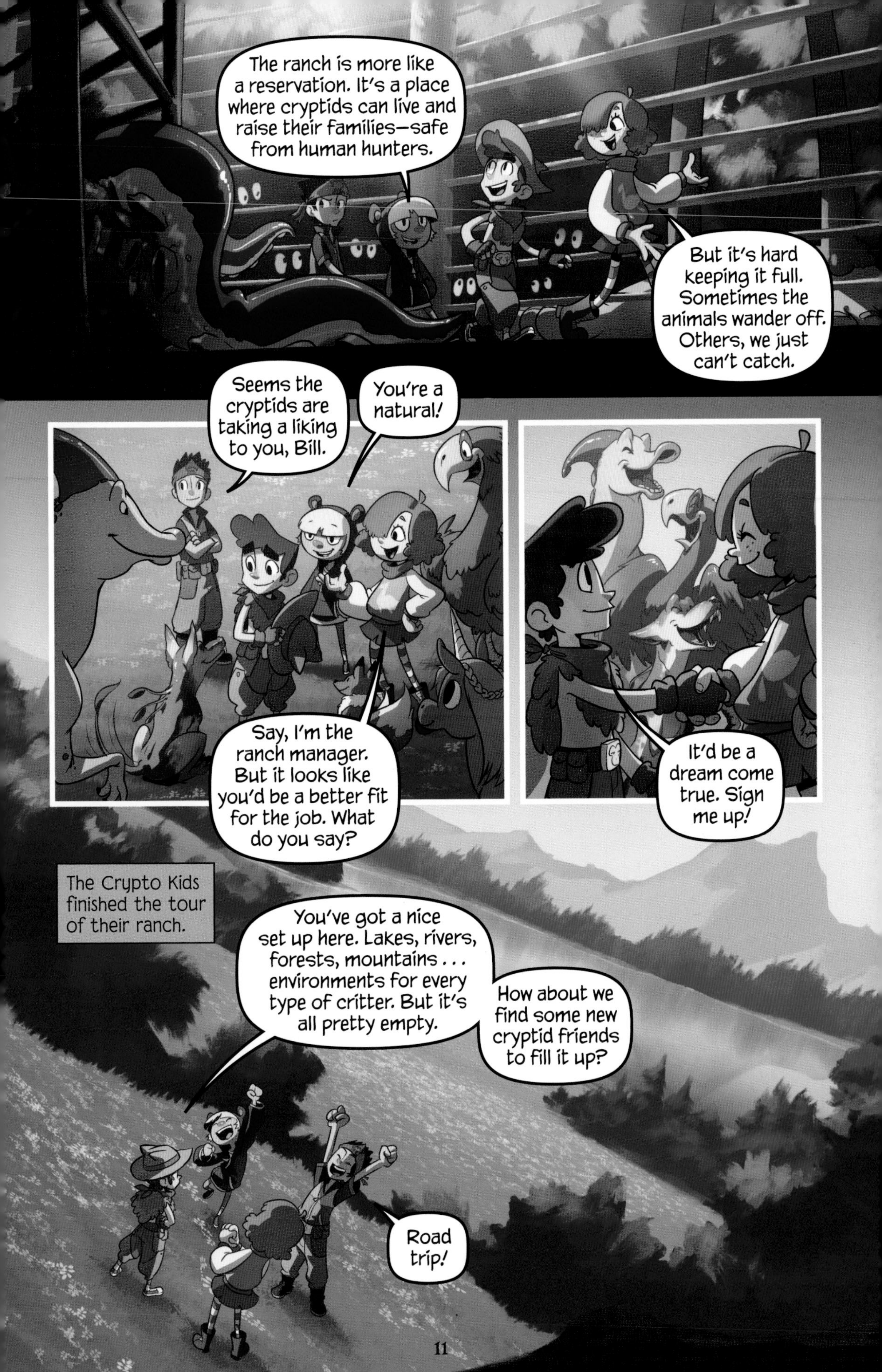
The ranch is more like a reservation. It's a place where cryptids can live and raise their families—safe from human hunters.
But it's hard keeping it full. Sometimes the animals wander off. Others, we just can't catch.
Seems the cryptids are taking a liking to you, Bill.
You're a natural!
Say, I'm the ranch manager. But it looks like you'd be a better fit for the job. What do you say?
It'd be a dream come true. Sign me up!
The Crypto Kids finished the tour of their ranch.
You've got a nice set up here. Lakes, rivers, forests, mountains . . . environments for every type of critter. But it's all pretty empty.
How about we find some new cryptid friends to fill it up?
Road trip!

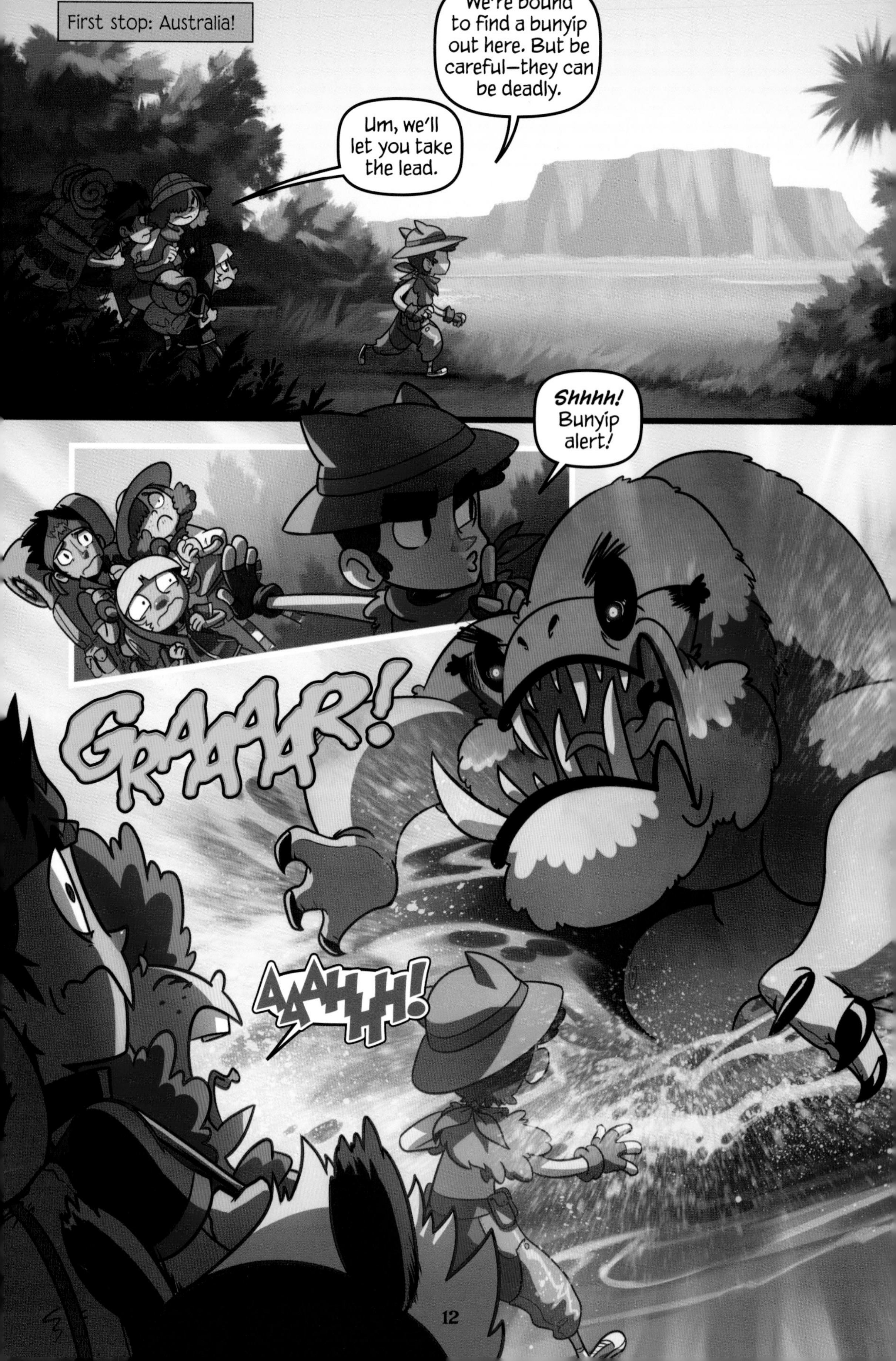
First stop: Australia!
We're bound to find a bunyip out here. But be careful—they can be deadly.
Um, we'll let you take the lead.
Shhhh! Bunyip alert!
GRAAAR!
AAAHHH!

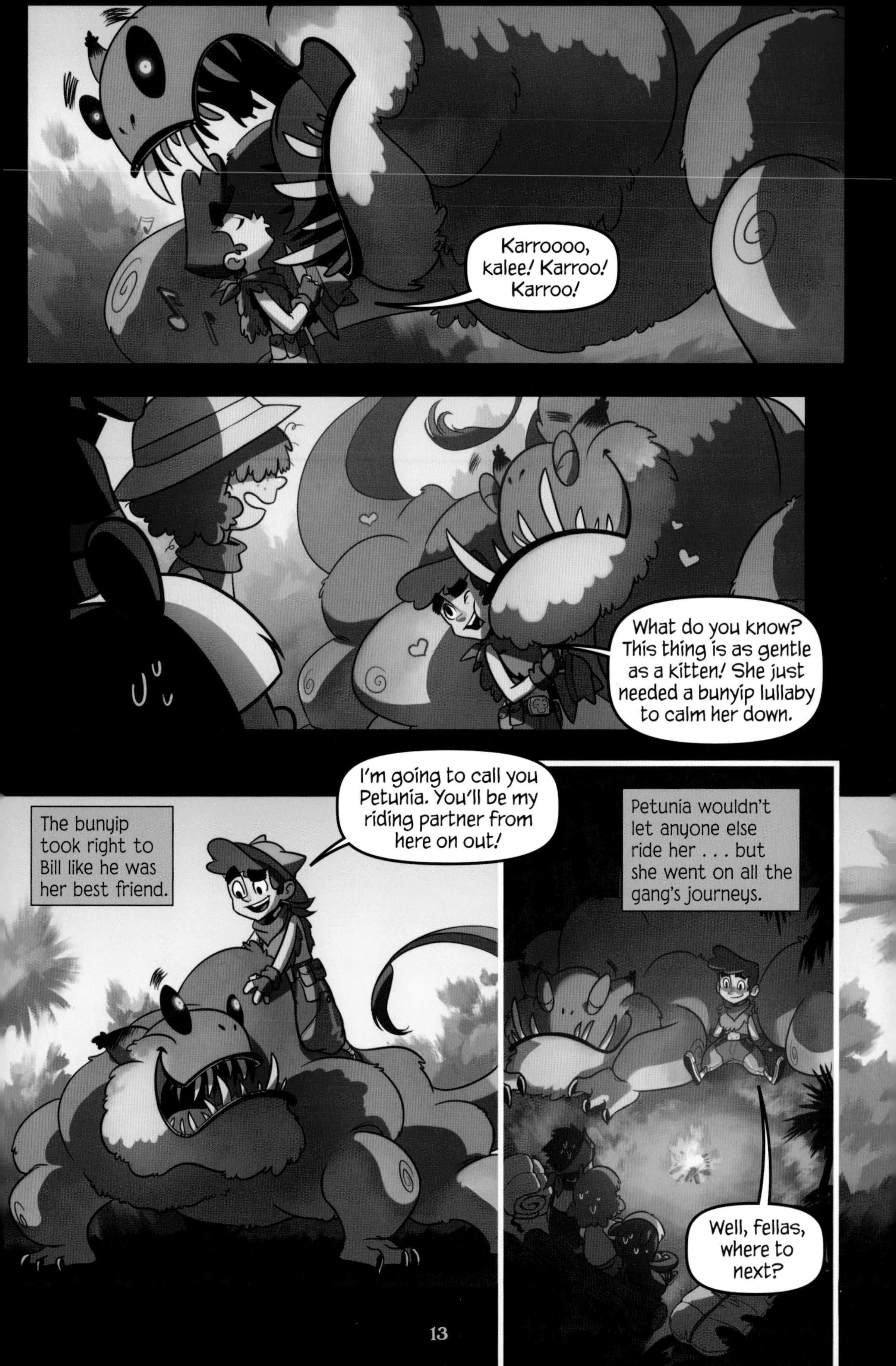

Karroooo, kalee! Karroo! Karroo!
What do you know? This thing is as gentle as a kitten! She just needed a bunyip lullaby to calm her down.
The bunyip took right to Bill like he was her best friend.
I'm going to call you Petunia. You'll be my riding partner from here on out!
Petunia wouldn't let anyone else ride her . . . but she went on all the gang's journeys.
Well, fellas, where to next?

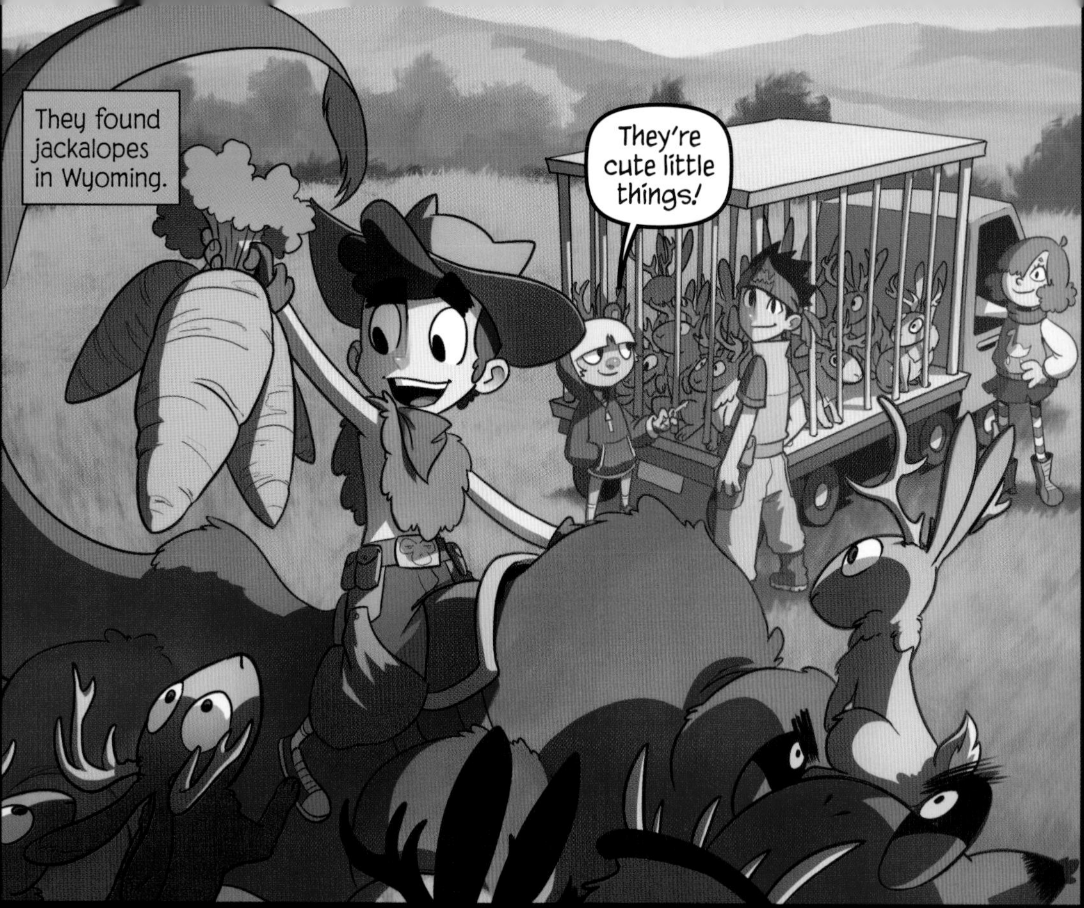
They found jackalopes in Wyoming.
They're cute little things!

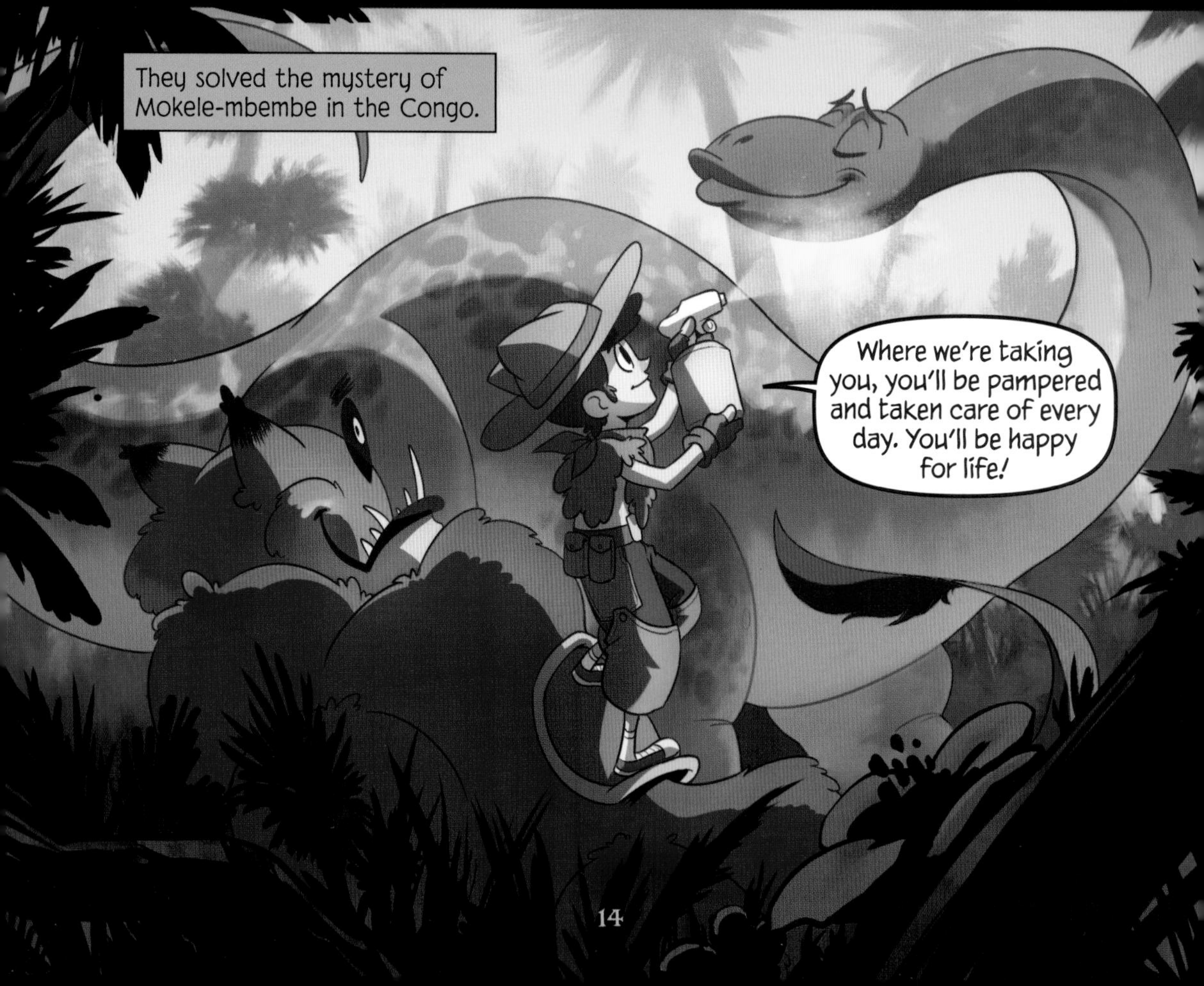
They solved the mystery of Mokele-mbembe in the Congo.
Where we're taking you, you'll be pampered and taken care of every day. You'll be happy for life!

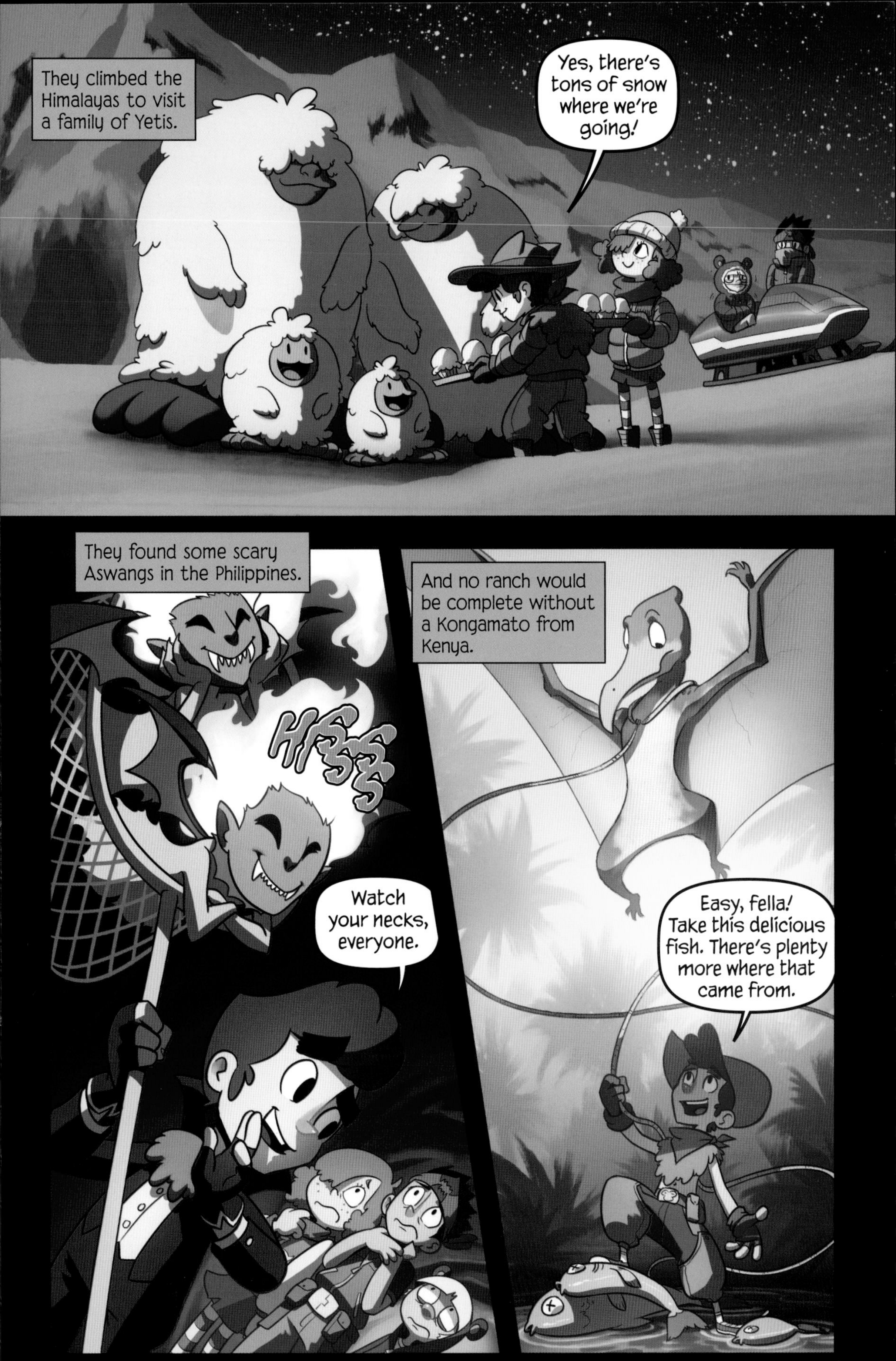
They climbed the Himalayas to visit a family of Yetis.
Yes, there's tons of snow where we're going!
They found some scary Aswangs in the Philippines.
HISSS
Watch your necks, everyone.
And no ranch would be complete without a Kongamato from Kenya.
Easy, fella! Take this delicious fish. There's plenty more where that came from.

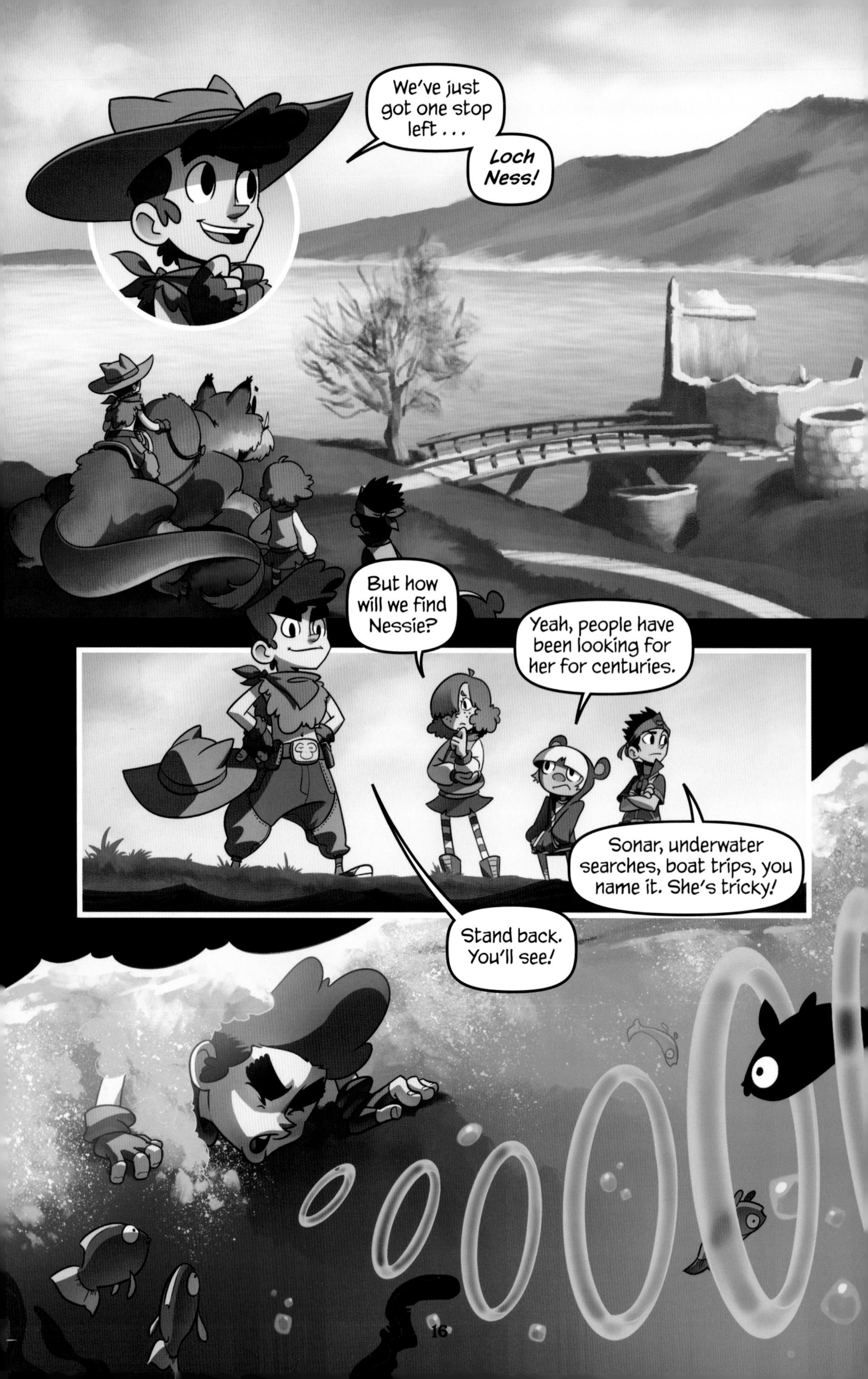
We've just got one stop left . . .
Loch Ness!
But how will we find Nessie?
Yeah, people have been looking for her for centuries.
Sonar, underwater searches, boat trips, you name it. She's tricky!
Stand back. You'll see!

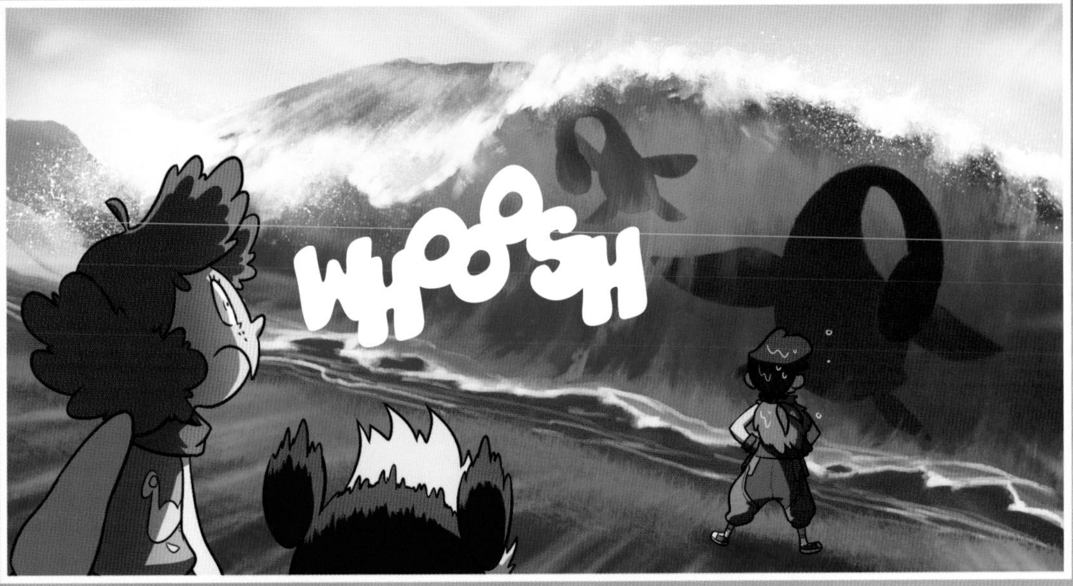
WHOOOSH

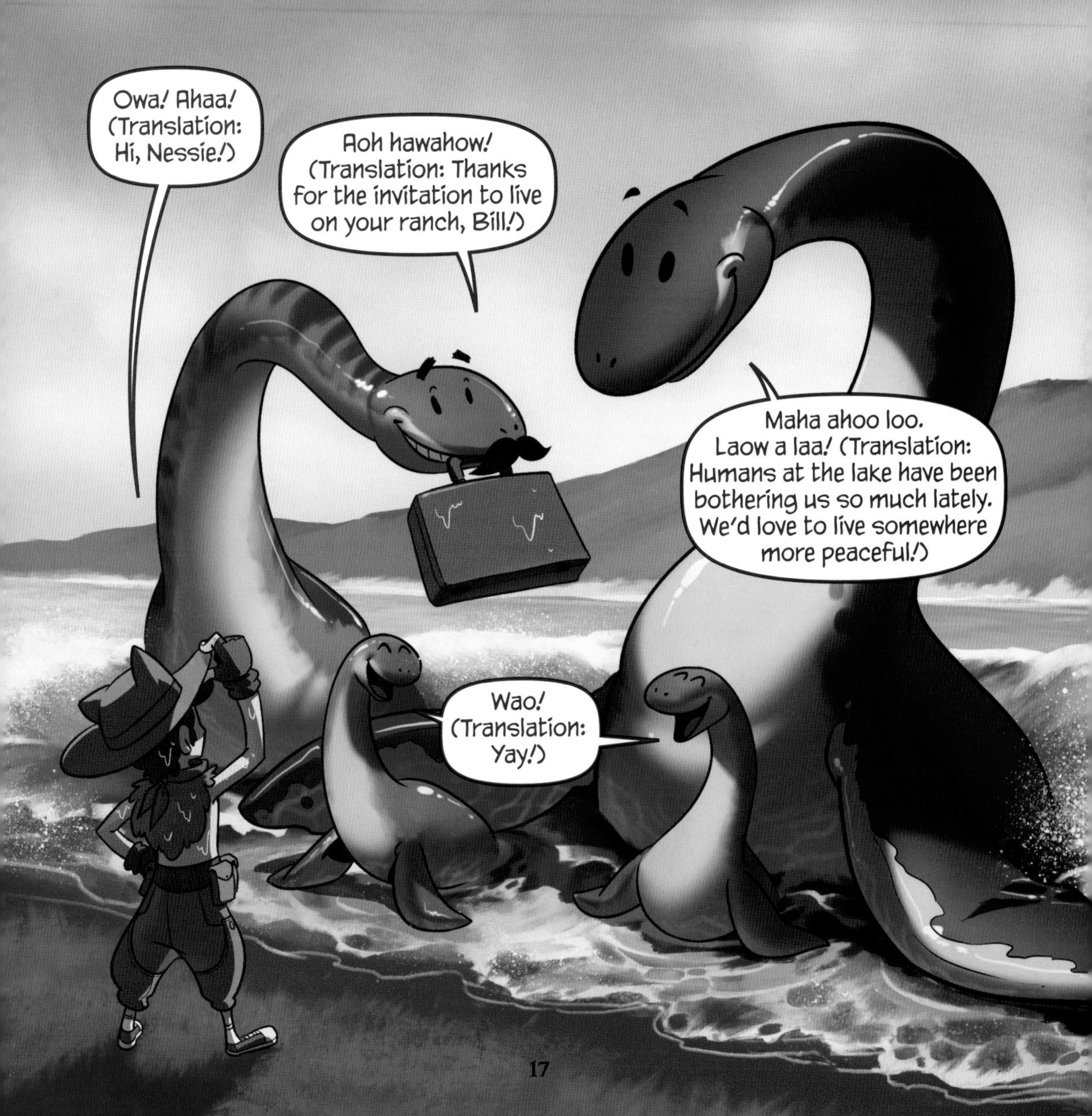
Owa! Ahaa! (Translation: Hi, Nessie!)
Aoh hawahow! (Translation: Thanks for the invitation to live on your ranch, Bill!)
Maha ahoo loo. Laow a laa! (Translation: Humans at the lake have been bothering us so much lately. We'd love to live somewhere more peaceful!)
Wao! (Translation: Yay!)

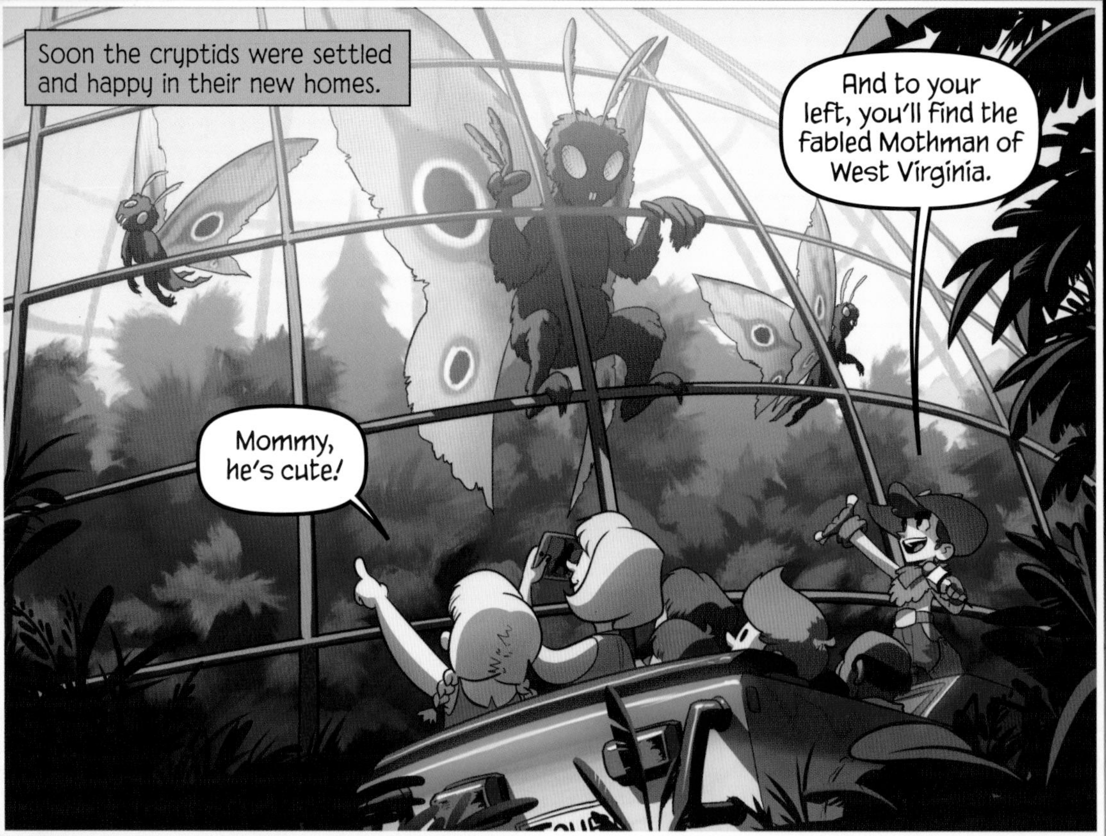
Soon the cryptids were settled and happy in their new homes.
And to your left, you'll find the fabled Mothman of West Virginia.
Mommy, he's cute!

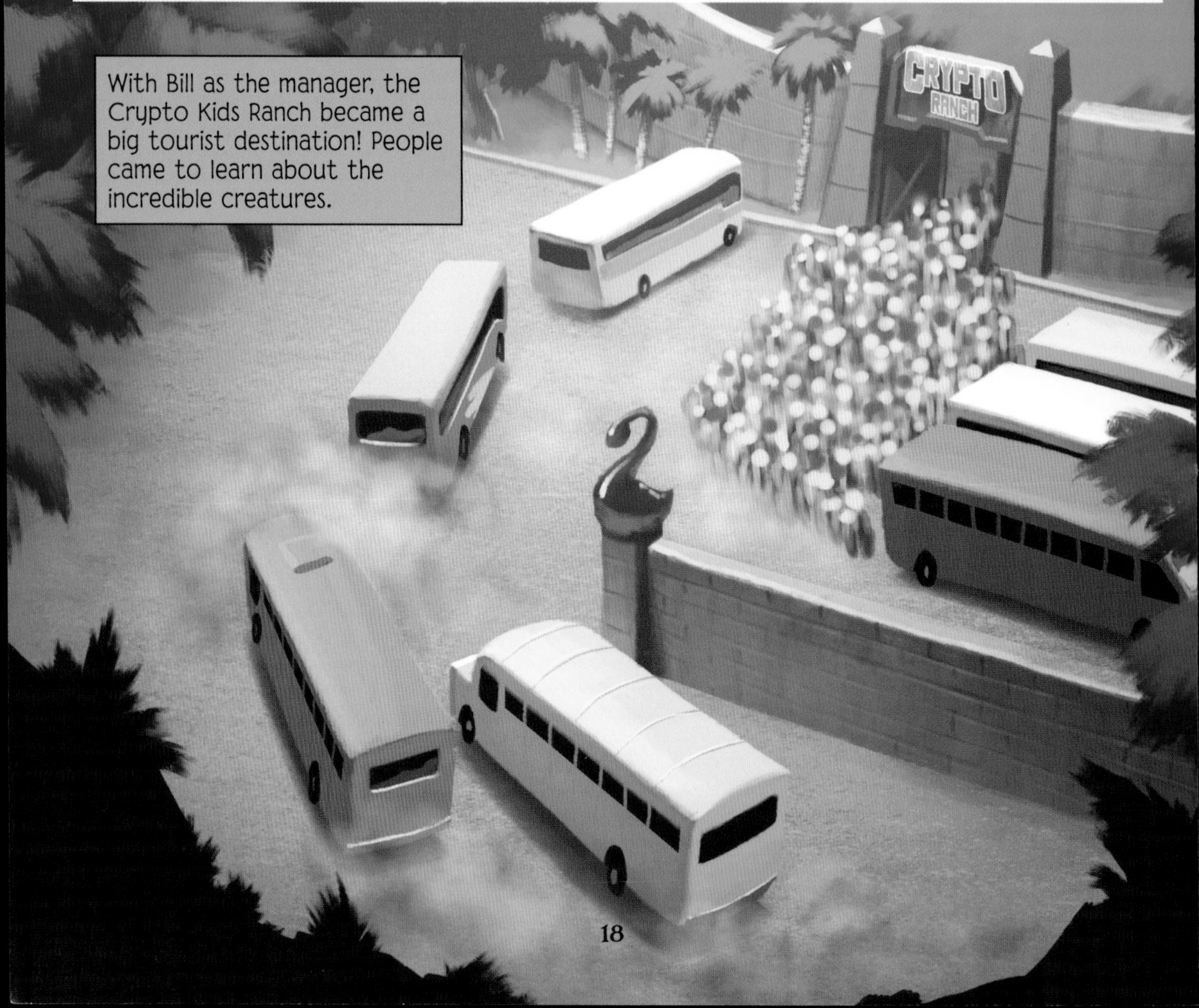
With Bill as the manager, the Crypto Kids Ranch became a big tourist destination! People came to learn about the incredible creatures.
CRYPTO RANCH

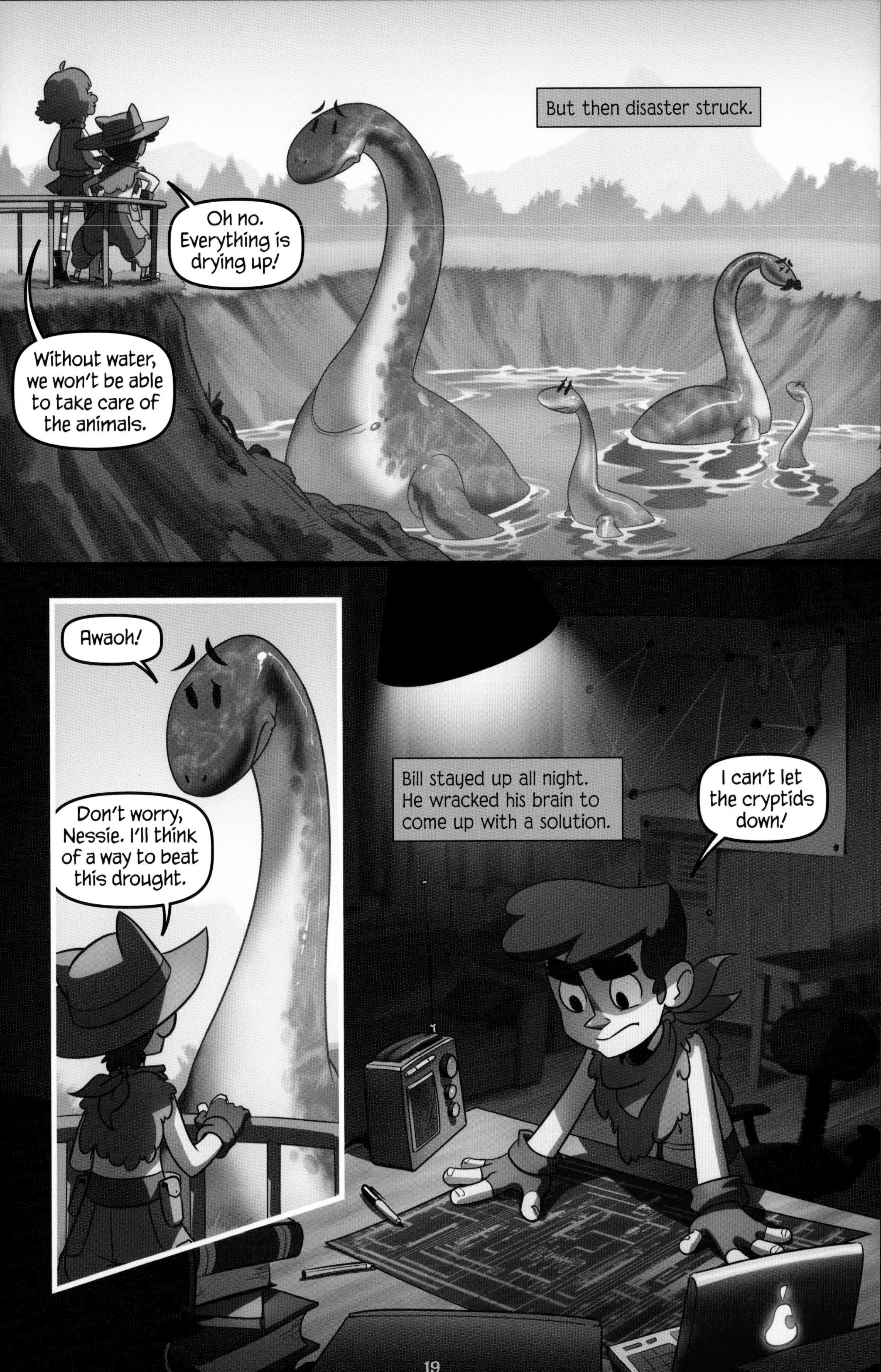

But then disaster struck.
Oh no. Everything is drying up!
Without water, we won't be able to take care of the animals.
Awaoh!
Don't worry, Nessie. I'll think of a way to beat this drought.
Bill stayed up all night. He wracked his brain to come up with a solution.
I can't let the cryptids down!

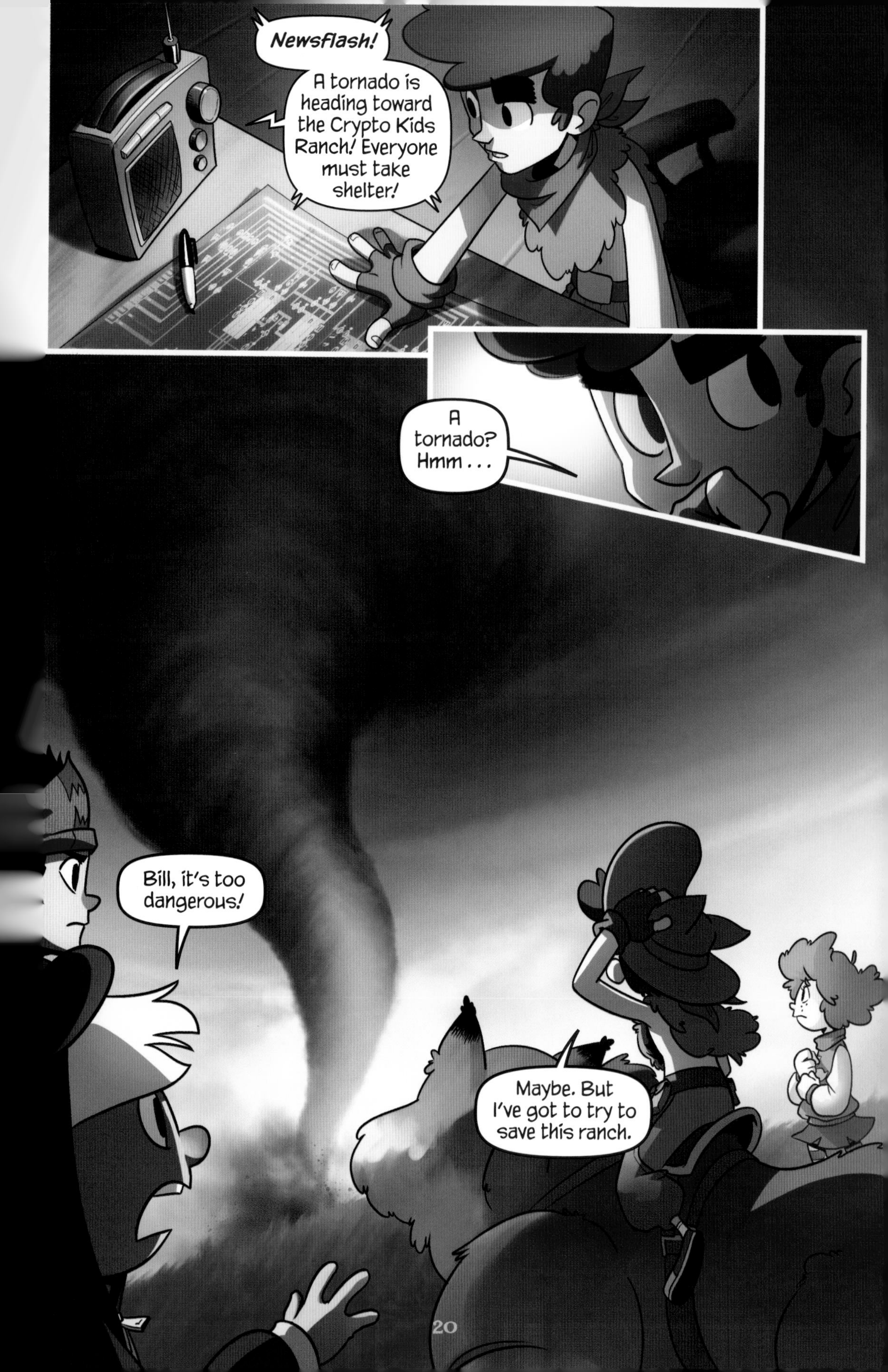
Newsflash!
A tornado is heading toward the Crypto Kids Ranch! Everyone must take shelter!
A tornado? Hmm . . .
Bill, it's too dangerous!
Maybe. But I've got to try to save this ranch.

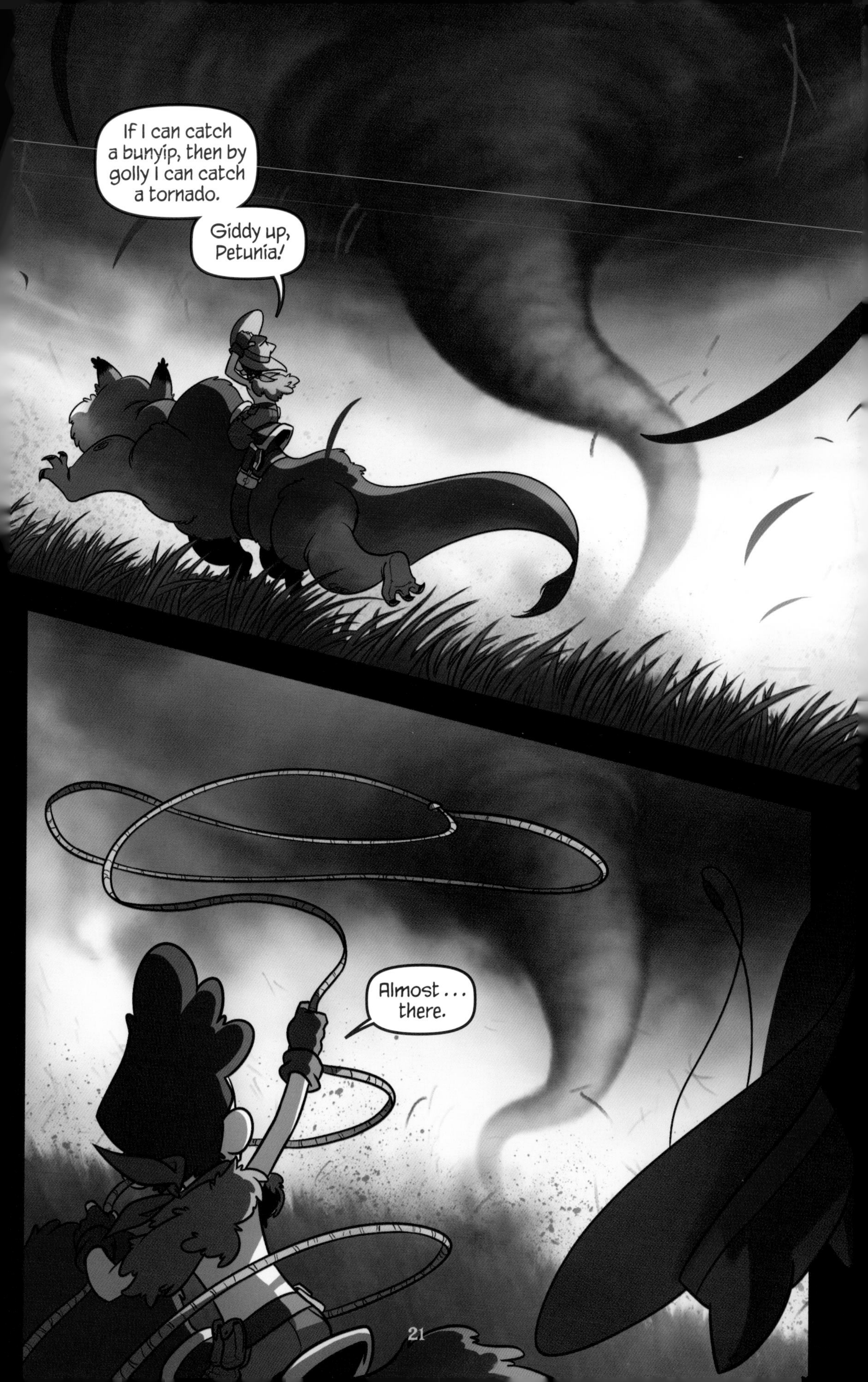
If I can catch a bunyip, then by golly I can catch a tornado.
Giddy up, Petunia!
Almost . . . there.

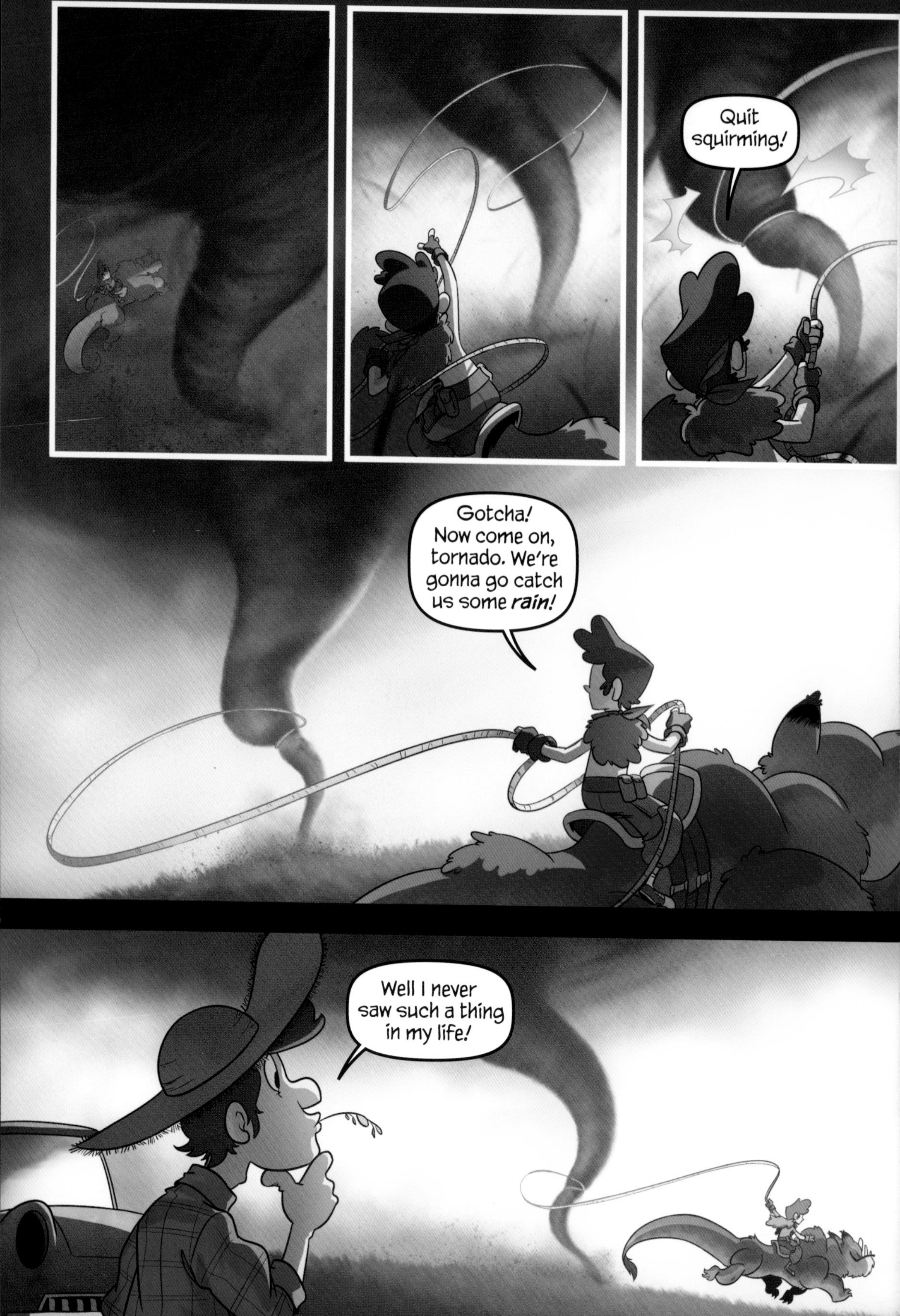
Quit squirming!
Gotcha! Now come on, tornado. We're gonna go catch us some *rain!*
Well I never saw such a thing in my life!

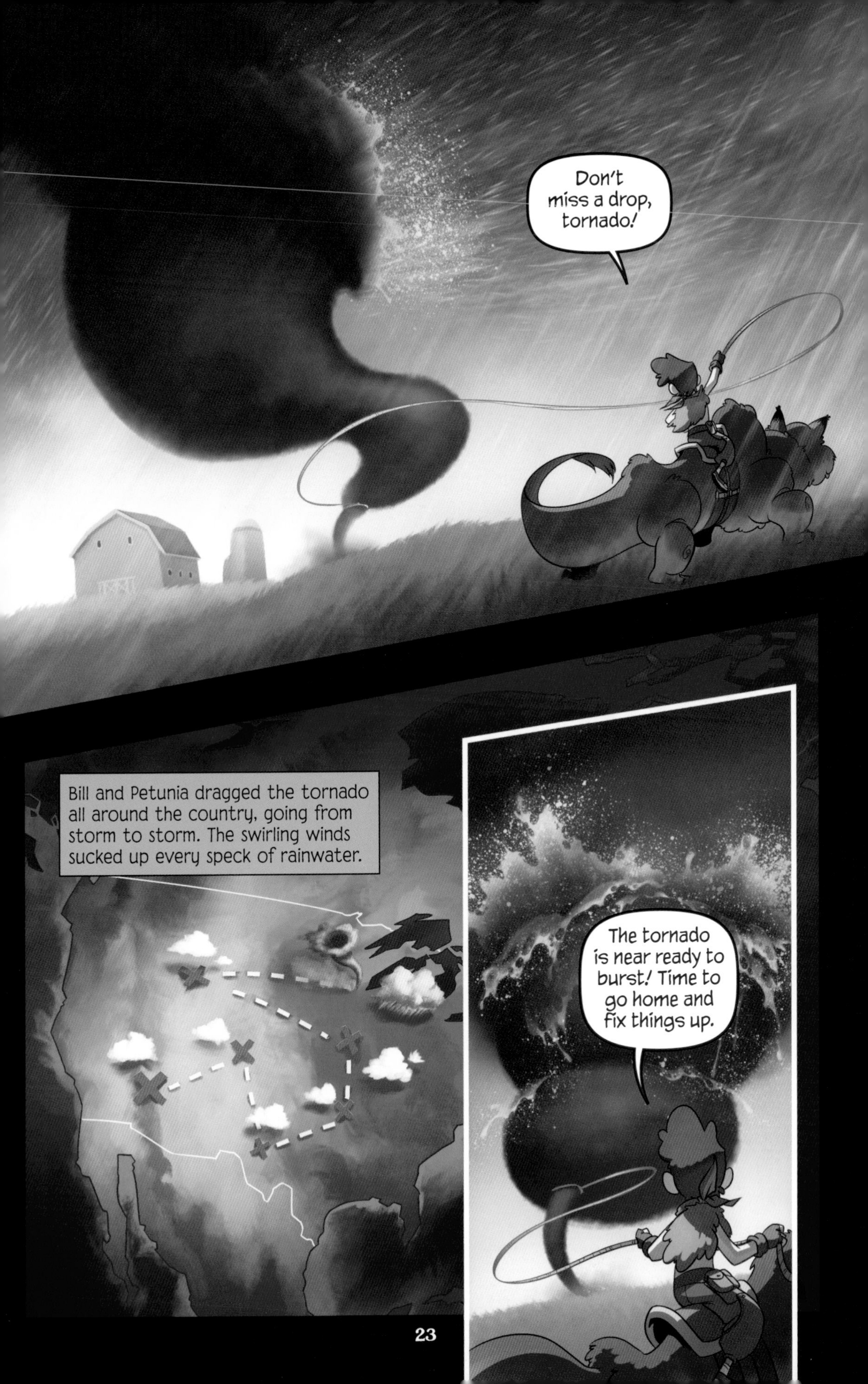
Don't miss a drop, tornado!
Bill and Petunia dragged the tornado all around the country, going from storm to storm. The swirling winds sucked up every speck of rainwater.
The tornado is near ready to burst! Time to go home and fix things up.

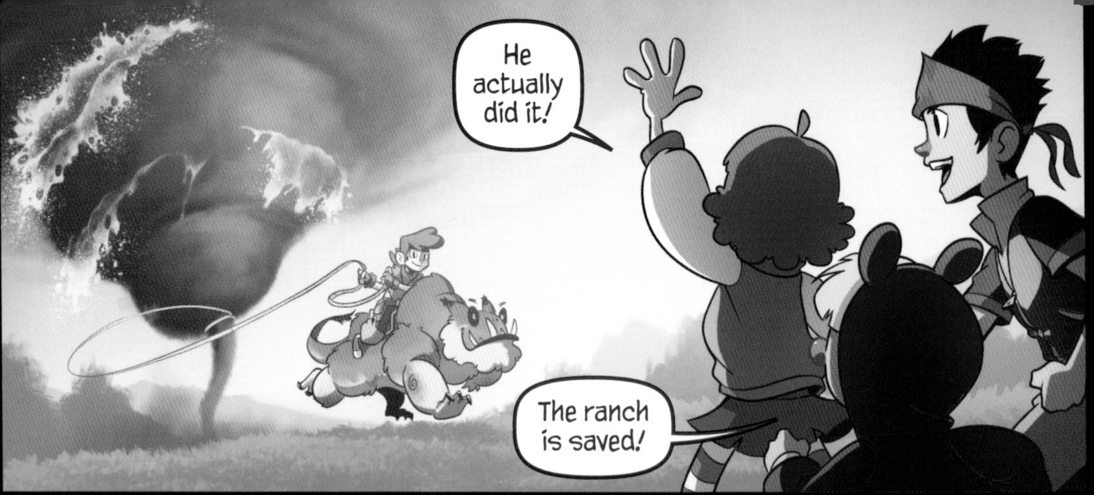
He actually did it!
The ranch is saved!

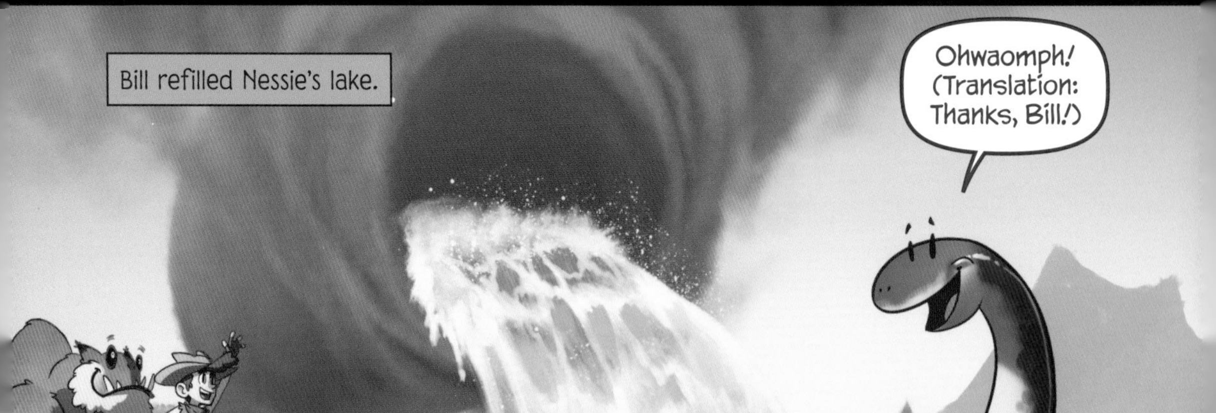
Bill refilled Nessie's lake.
Ohwaomph! (Translation: Thanks, Bill!)

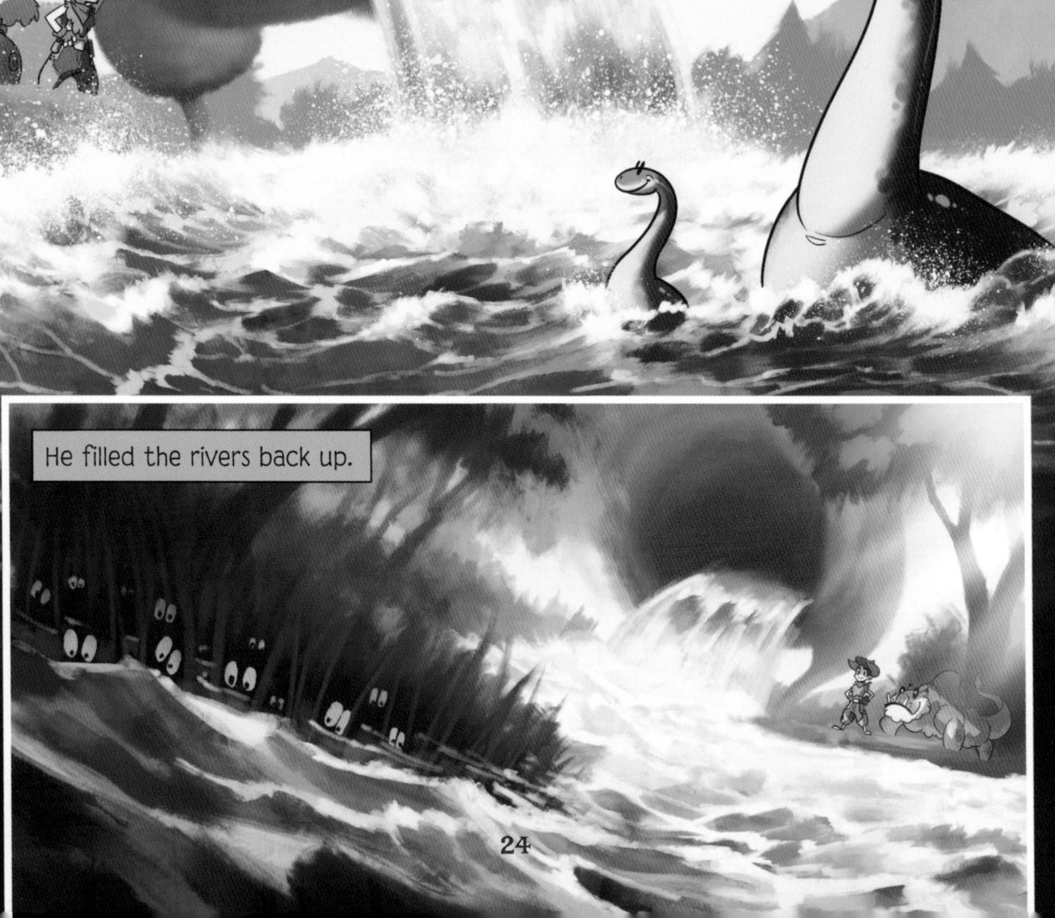
He filled the rivers back up.

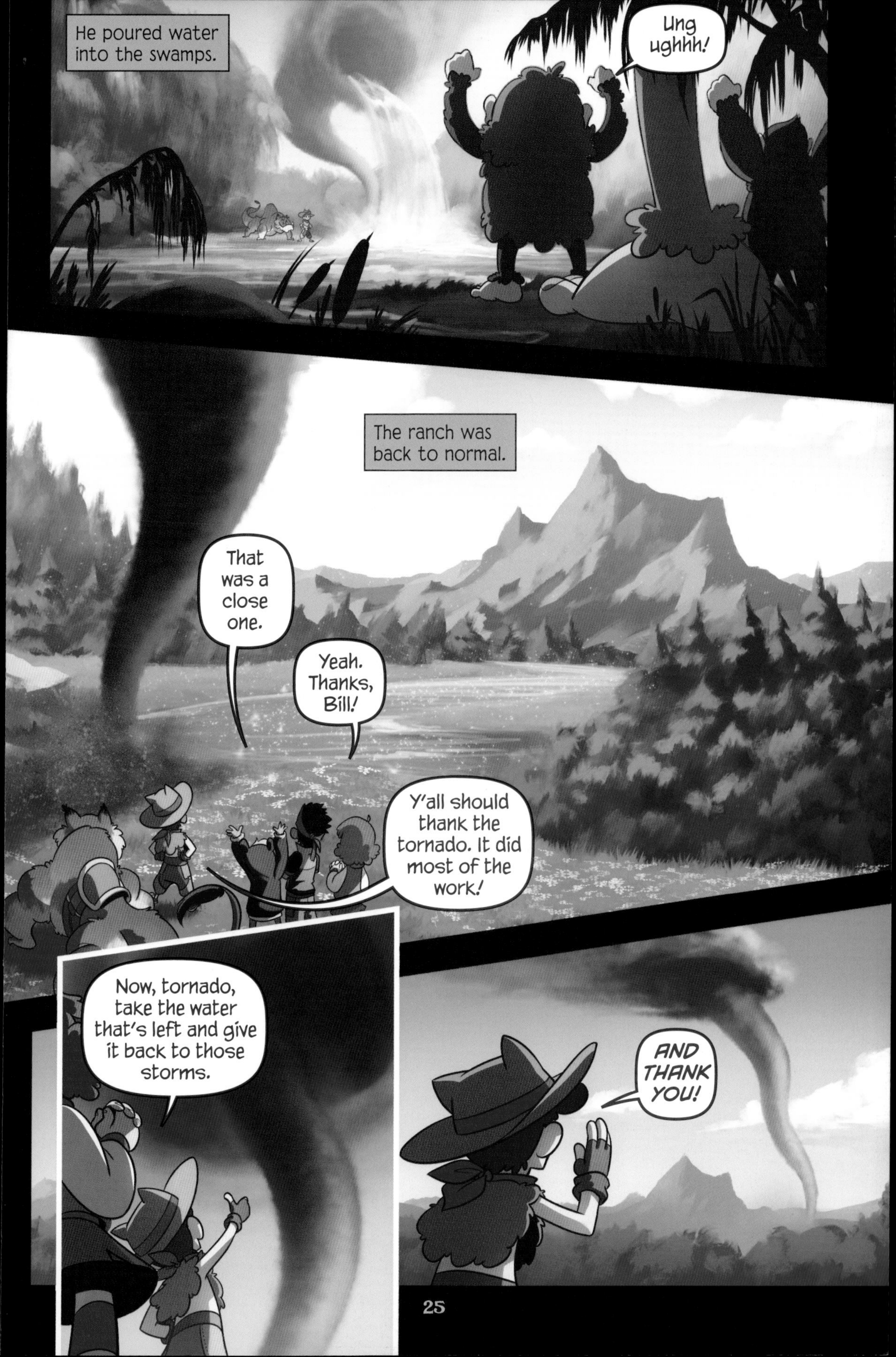
He poured water into the swamps.
Ung ughhh!
The ranch was back to normal.
That was a close one.
Yeah. Thanks, Bill!
Y'all should thank the tornado. It did most of the work!
Now, tornado, take the water that's left and give it back to those storms.
AND THANK YOU!

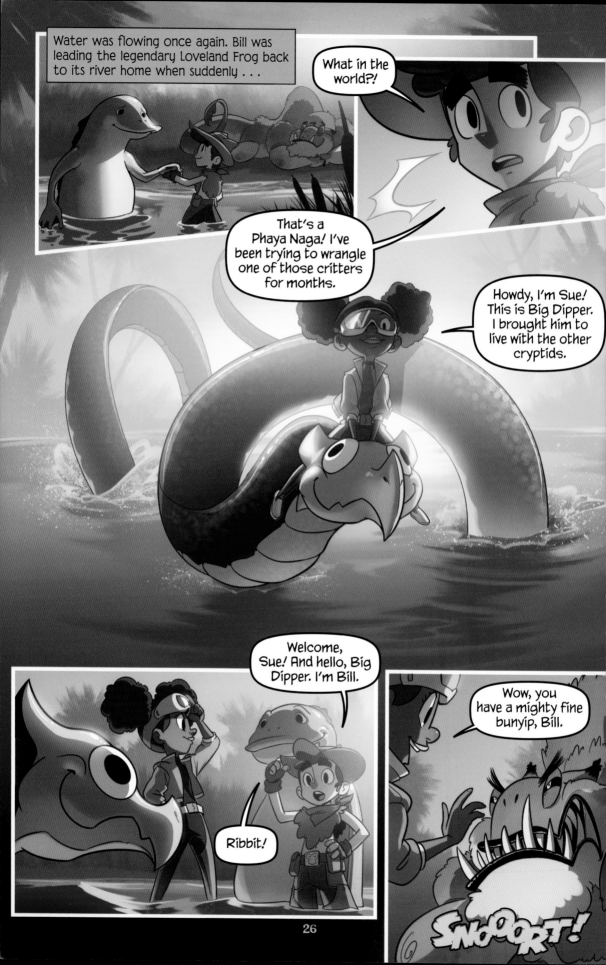

Water was flowing once again. Bill was leading the legendary Loveland Frog back to its river home when suddenly . . .

What in the world?!

That's a Phaya Naga! I've been trying to wrangle one of those critters for months.

Howdy, I'm Sue! This is Big Dipper. I brought him to live with the other cryptids.

Welcome, Sue! And hello, Big Dipper. I'm Bill.

Ribbit!

Wow, you have a mighty fine bunyip, Bill.

SNOOORT!

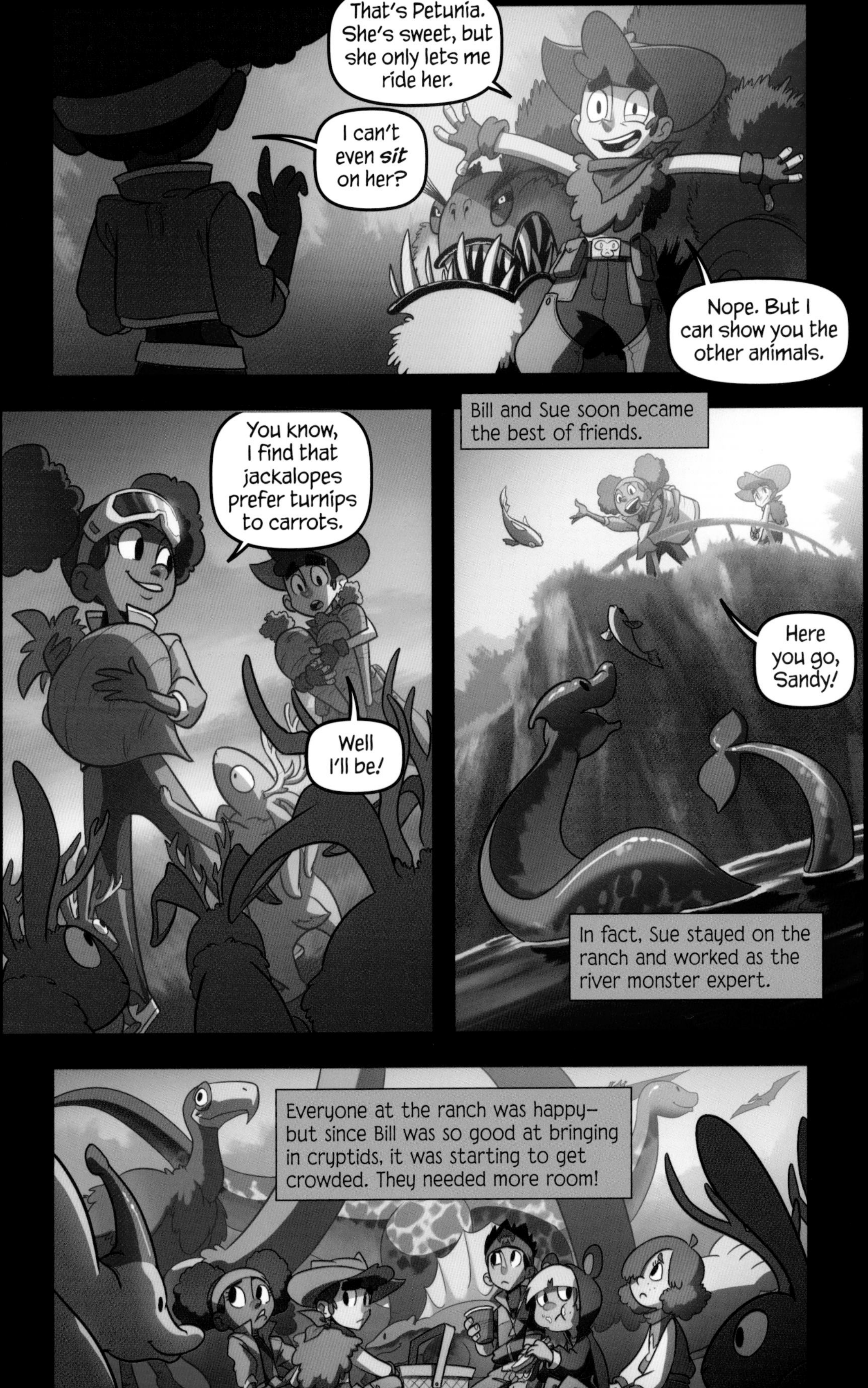

That's Petunia. She's sweet, but she only lets me ride her.
I can't even *sit* on her?
Nope. But I can show you the other animals.
You know, I find that jackalopes prefer turnips to carrots.
Well I'll be!
Bill and Sue soon became the best of friends.
Here you go, Sandy!
In fact, Sue stayed on the ranch and worked as the river monster expert.
Everyone at the ranch was happy—but since Bill was so good at bringing in cryptids, it was starting to get crowded. They needed more room!

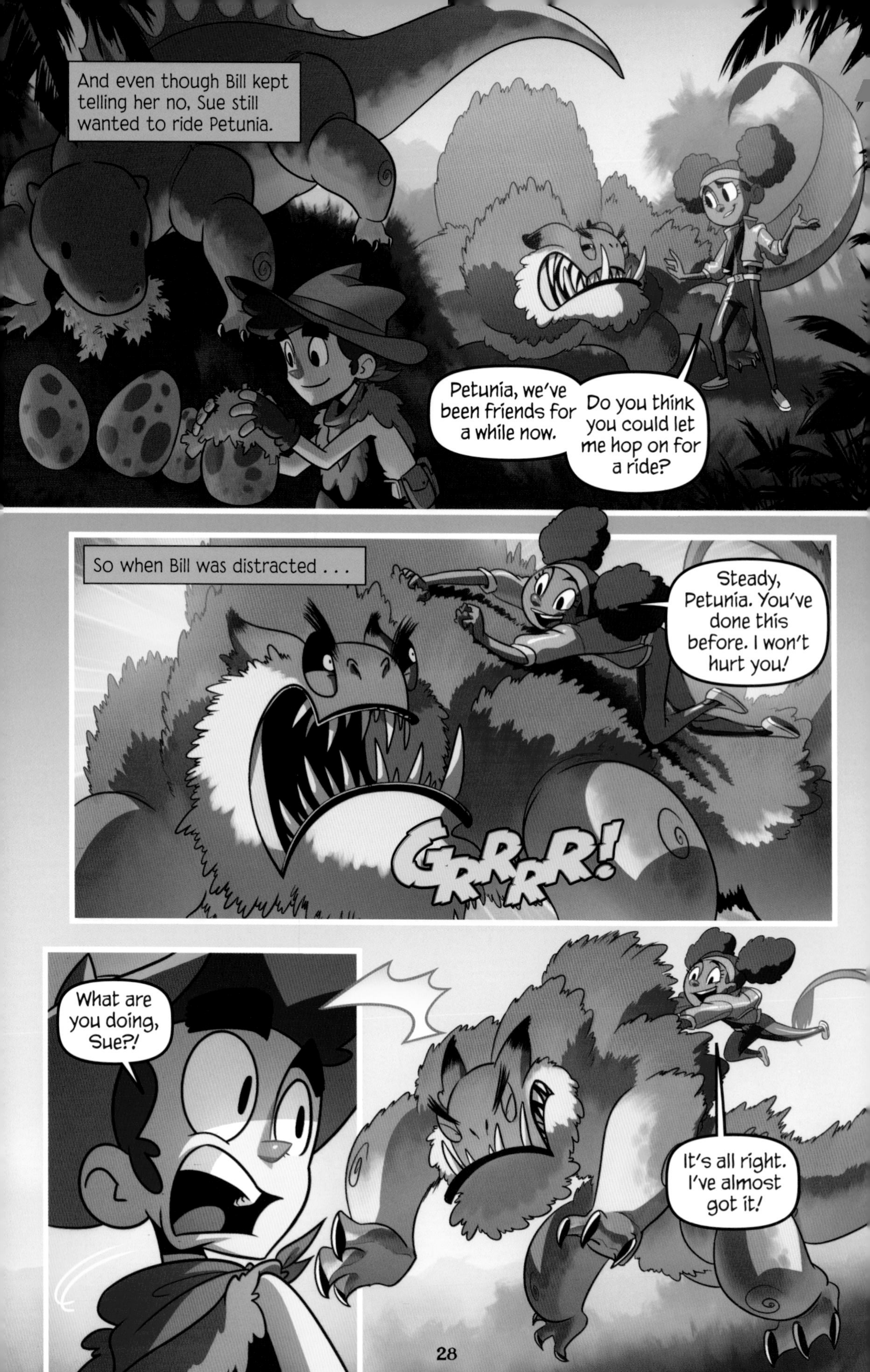
And even though Bill kept telling her no, Sue still wanted to ride Petunia.
Petunia, we've been friends for a while now.
Do you think you could let me hop on for a ride?
So when Bill was distracted . . .
Steady, Petunia. You've done this before. I won't hurt you!
GRRRR!
What are you doing, Sue?!
It's all right. I've almost got it!

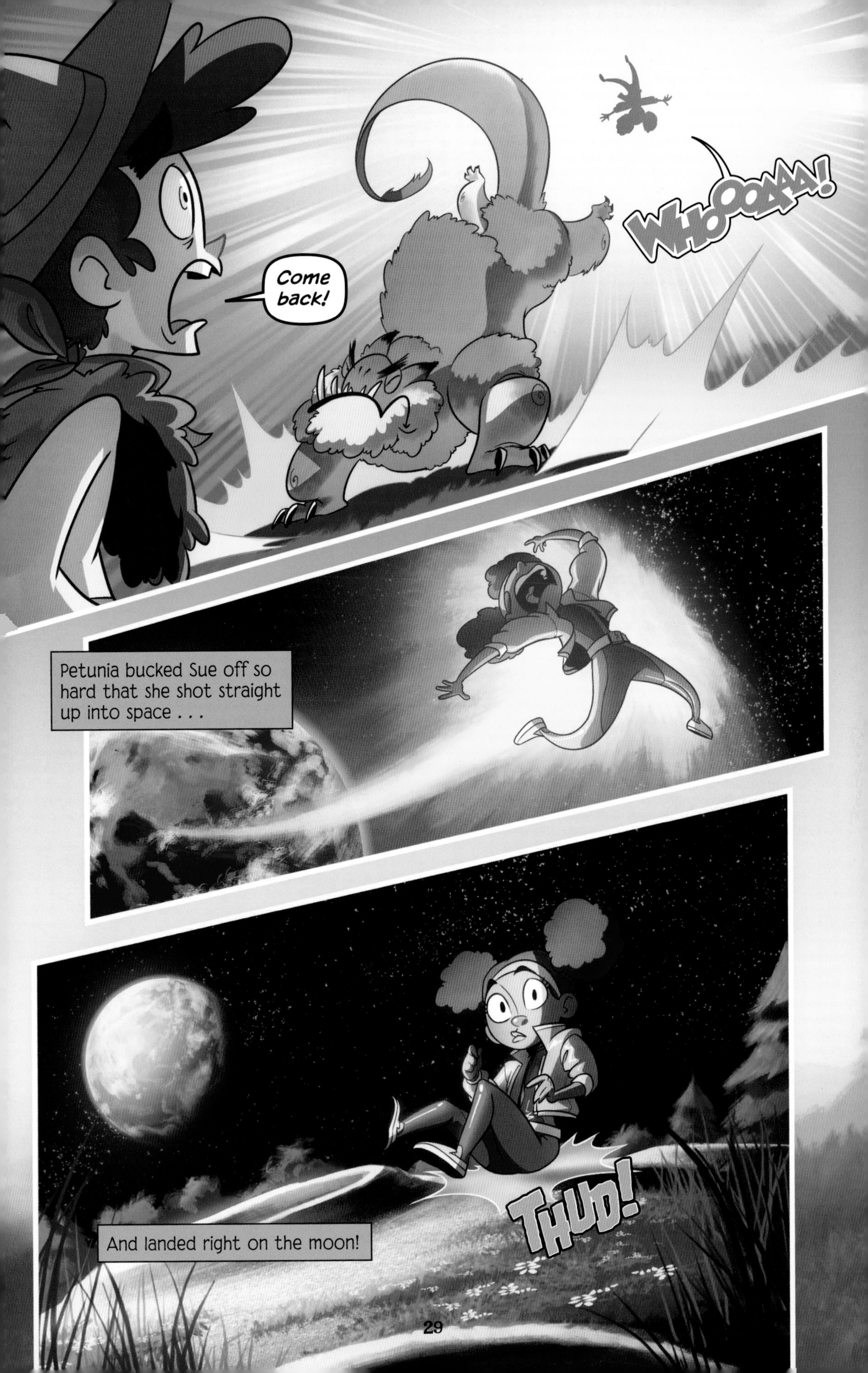
Come back!
WHOOOAAA!
Petunia bucked Sue off so hard that she shot straight up into space . . .
THUD!
And landed right on the moon!

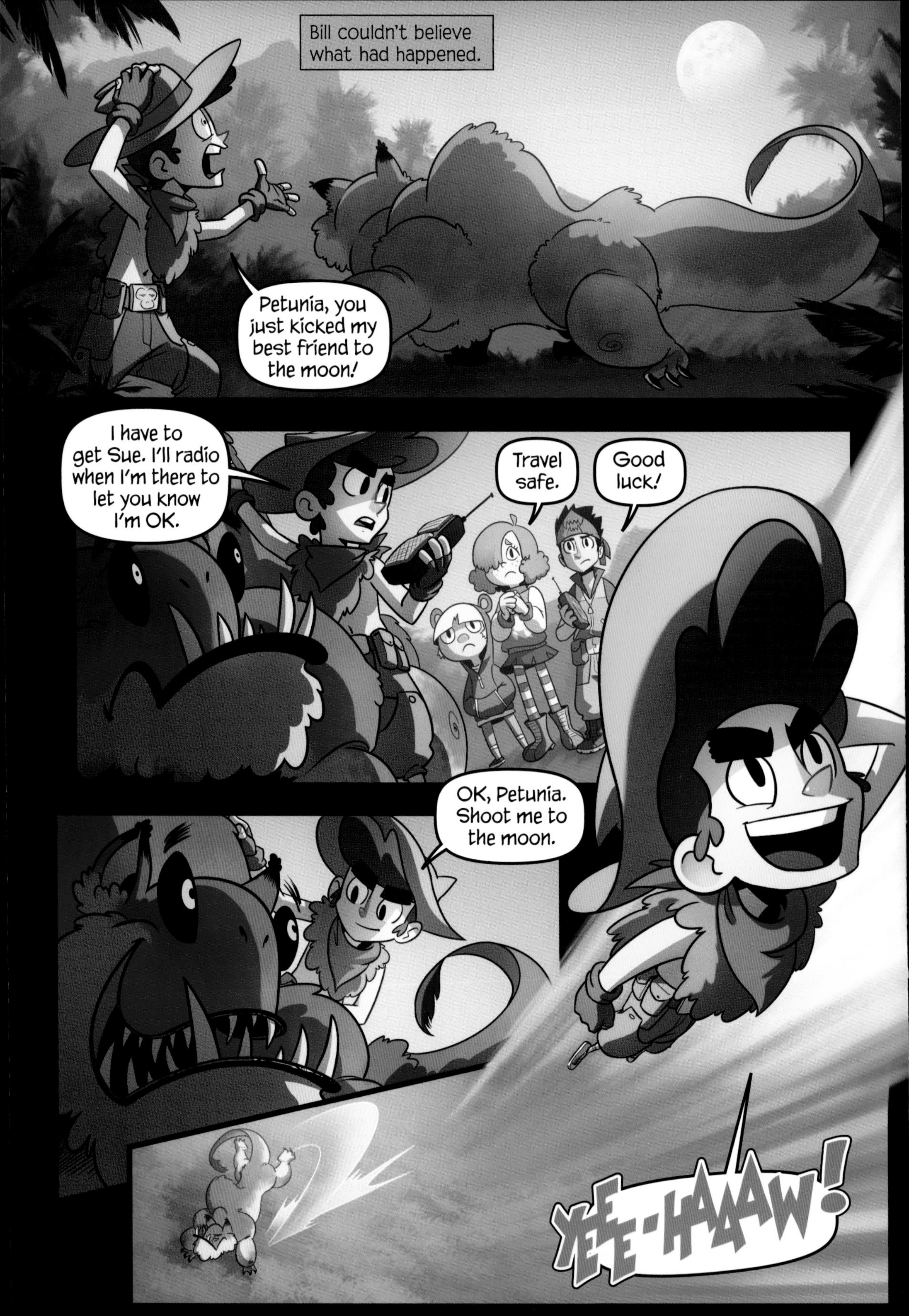
Bill couldn't believe what had happened.
Petunia, you just kicked my best friend to the moon!
I have to get Sue. I'll radio when I'm there to let you know I'm OK.
Travel safe.
Good luck!
OK, Petunia. Shoot me to the moon.
YEE-HAAAW!

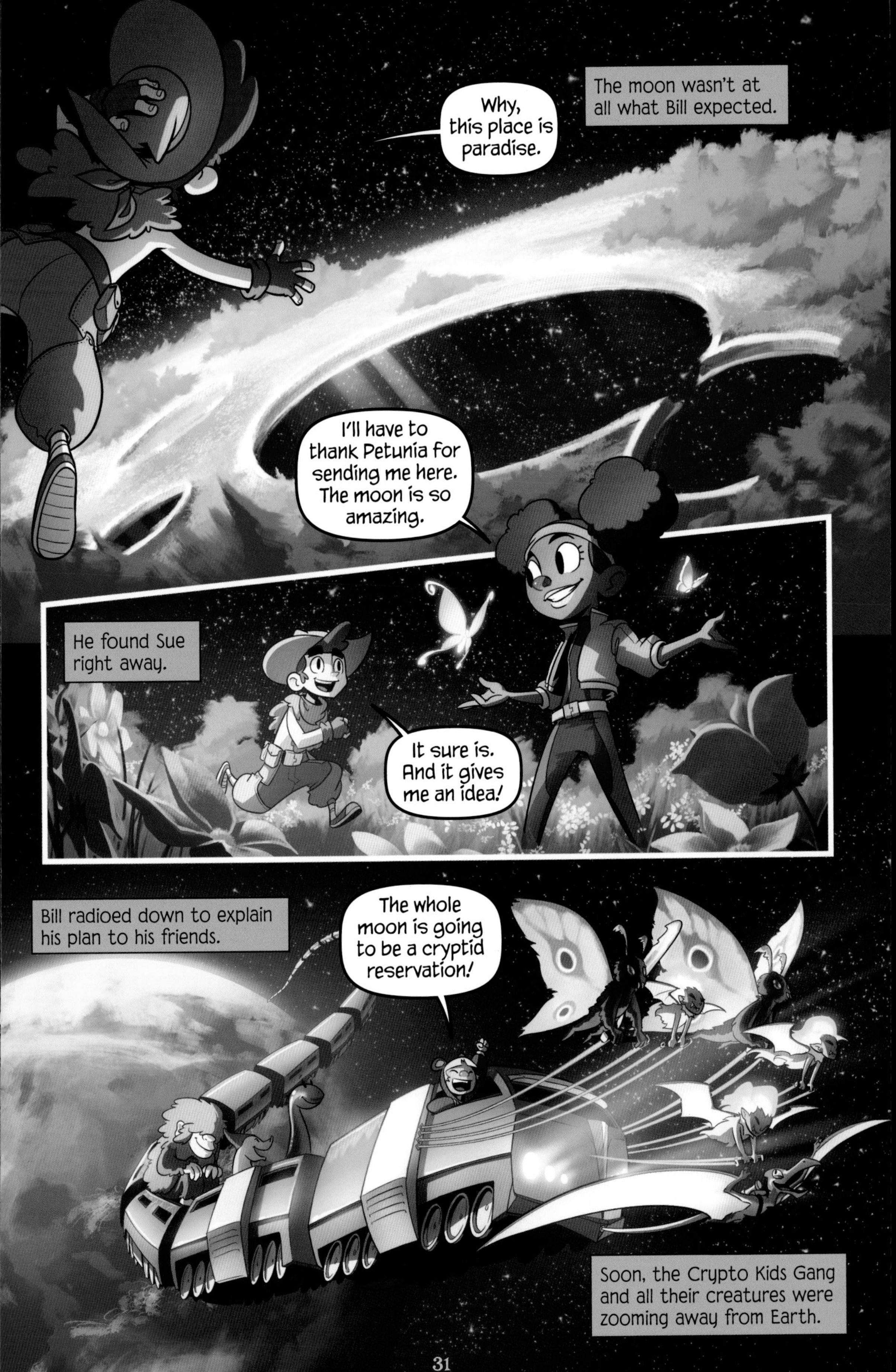

The moon wasn't at all what Bill expected.
Why, this place is paradise.
I'll have to thank Petunia for sending me here. The moon is so amazing.
He found Sue right away.
It sure is. And it gives me an idea!
Bill radioed down to explain his plan to his friends.
The whole moon is going to be a cryptid reservation!
Soon, the Crypto Kids Gang and all their creatures were zooming away from Earth.

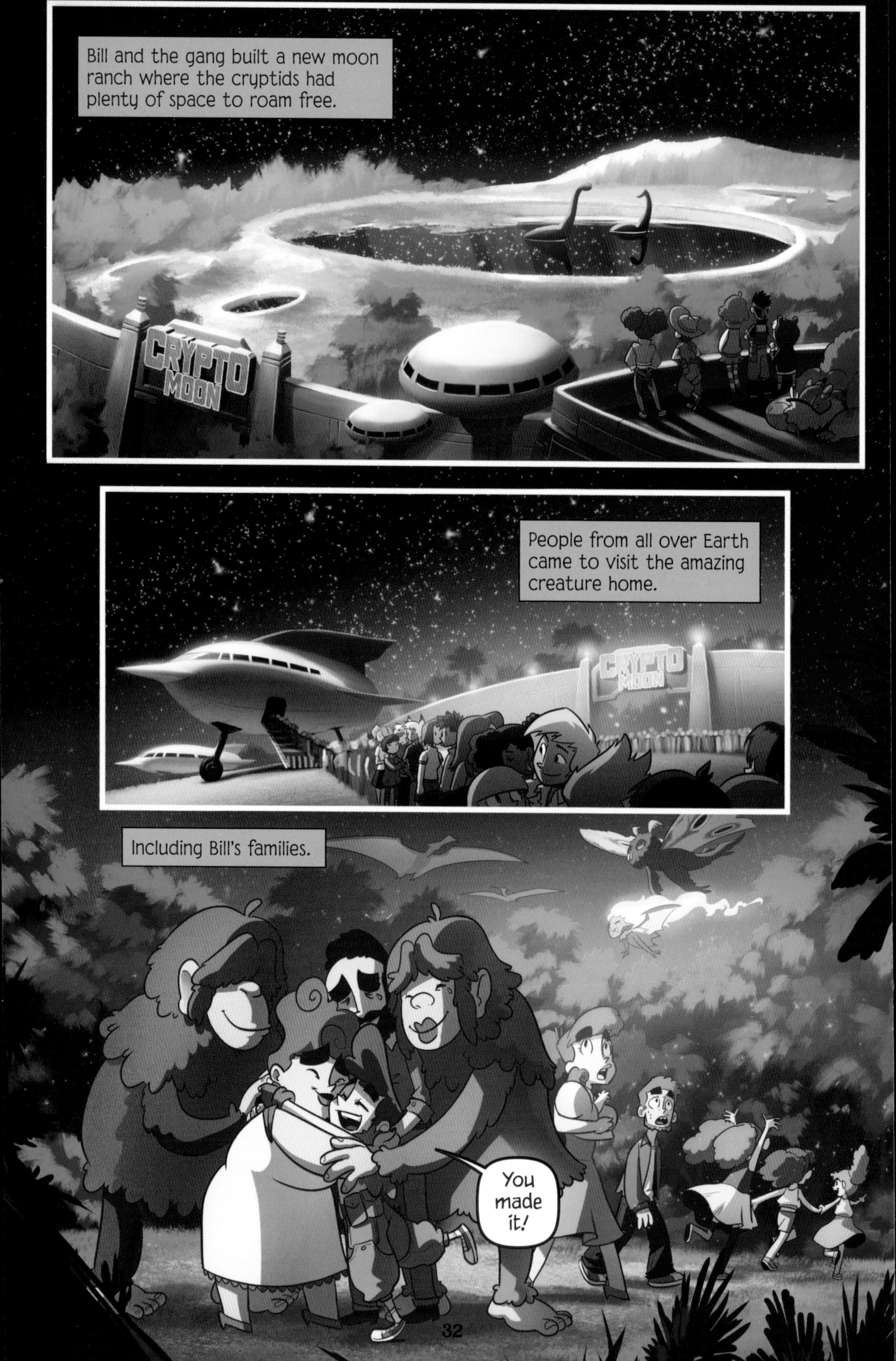
Bill and the gang built a new moon ranch where the cryptids had plenty of space to roam free.
CRYPTO MOON
People from all over Earth came to visit the amazing creature home.
CRYPTO MOON
Including Bill's families.
You made it!

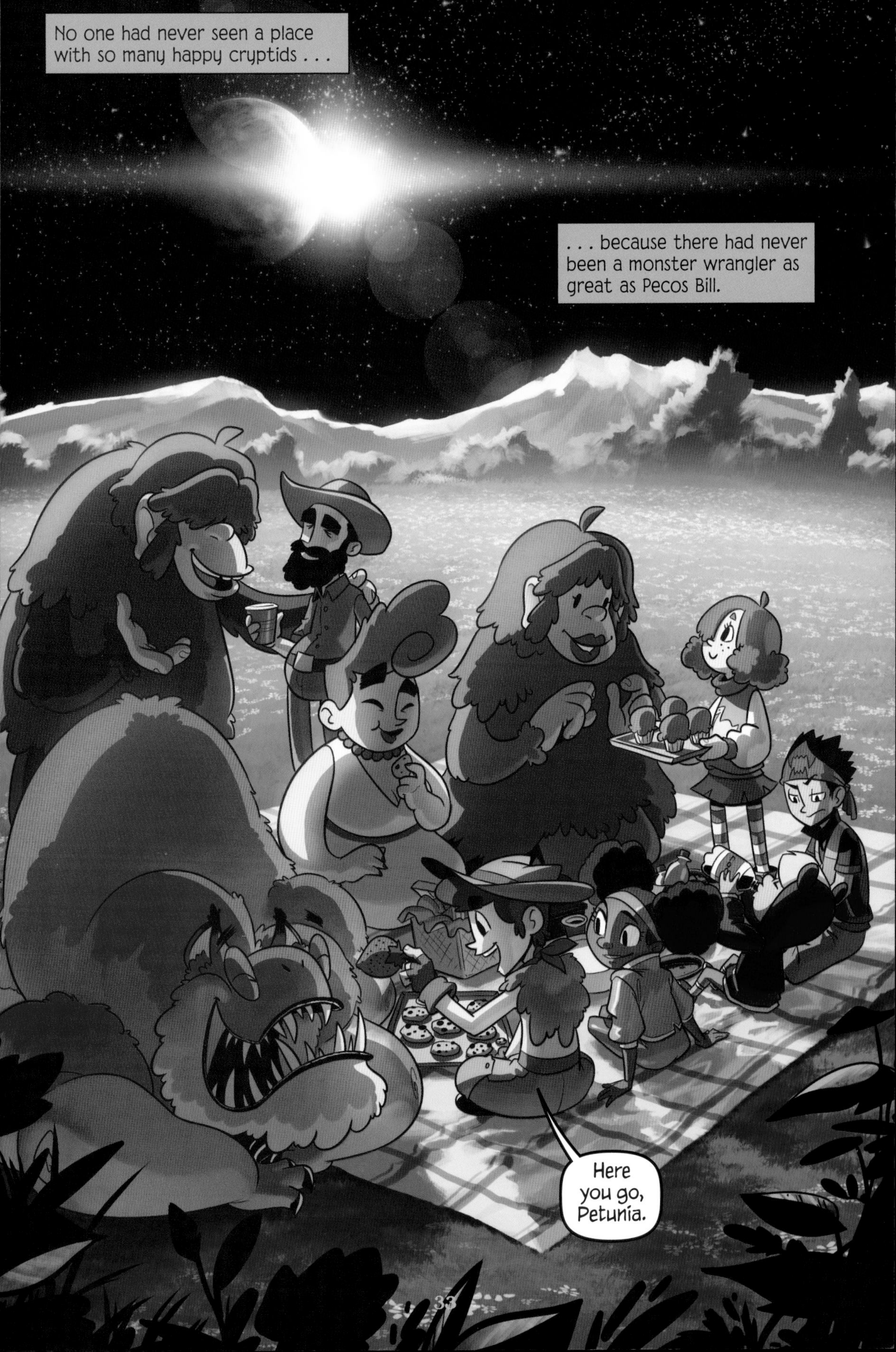
No one had never seen a place with so many happy cryptids . . .
. . . because there had never been a monster wrangler as great as Pecos Bill.
Here you go, Petunia.

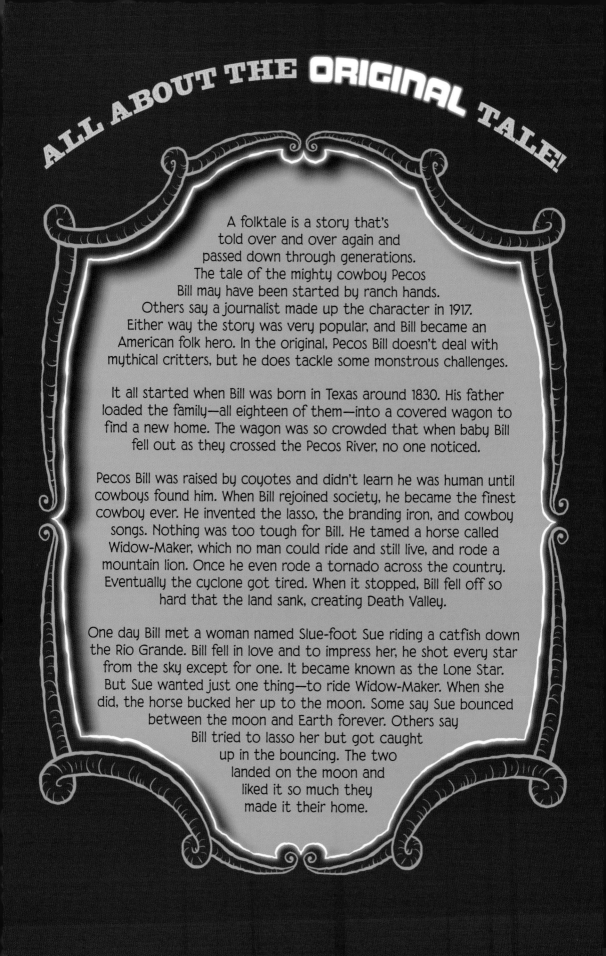

ALL ABOUT THE ORIGINAL TALE!

A folktale is a story that's told over and over again and passed down through generations. The tale of the mighty cowboy Pecos Bill may have been started by ranch hands. Others say a journalist made up the character in 1917. Either way the story was very popular, and Bill became an American folk hero. In the original, Pecos Bill doesn't deal with mythical critters, but he does tackle some monstrous challenges.

It all started when Bill was born in Texas around 1830. His father loaded the family—all eighteen of them—into a covered wagon to find a new home. The wagon was so crowded that when baby Bill fell out as they crossed the Pecos River, no one noticed.

Pecos Bill was raised by coyotes and didn't learn he was human until cowboys found him. When Bill rejoined society, he became the finest cowboy ever. He invented the lasso, the branding iron, and cowboy songs. Nothing was too tough for Bill. He tamed a horse called Widow-Maker, which no man could ride and still live, and rode a mountain lion. Once he even rode a tornado across the country. Eventually the cyclone got tired. When it stopped, Bill fell off so hard that the land sank, creating Death Valley.

One day Bill met a woman named Slue-foot Sue riding a catfish down the Rio Grande. Bill fell in love and to impress her, he shot every star from the sky except for one. It became known as the Lone Star. But Sue wanted just one thing—to ride Widow-Maker. When she did, the horse bucked her up to the moon. Some say Sue bounced between the moon and Earth forever. Others say Bill tried to lasso her but got caught up in the bouncing. The two landed on the moon and liked it so much they made it their home.

A **FAR OUT** GUIDE TO THE TALE'S CRYPTID TWISTS!

In this version, Pecos Bill isn't a cowboy raised by coyotes. He's a monster wrangler raised by friendly Sasquatches!

Bill's wild horse is replaced with a fierce (but lovable!) bunyip.

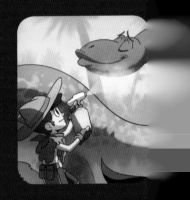

Instead of using his skills to tame the Wild West, Bill helps protect and care for creatures.

In the original, Sue bounces between the moon and Earth. Here the whole gang goes to the moon and it becomes a cryptid home!

VISUAL QUESTIONS

How do you think Bill felt about leaving his Sasquatch family? Use examples from the art and text to support your answer.

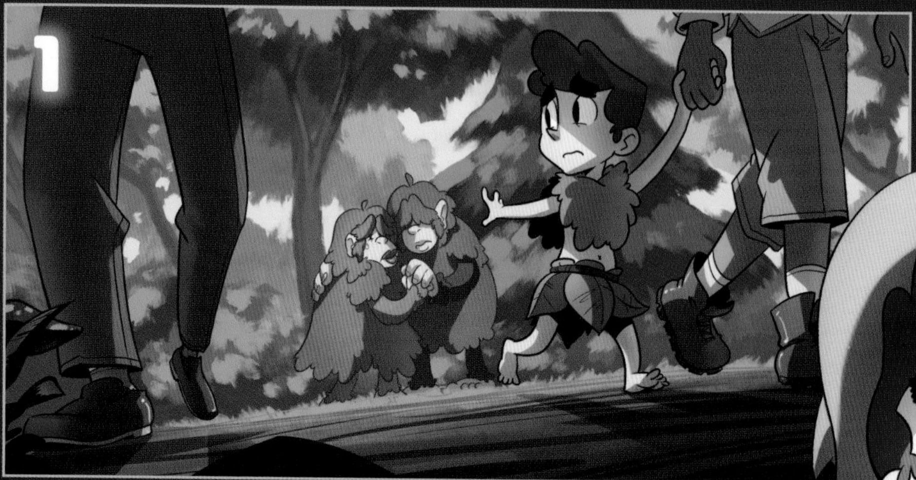
1

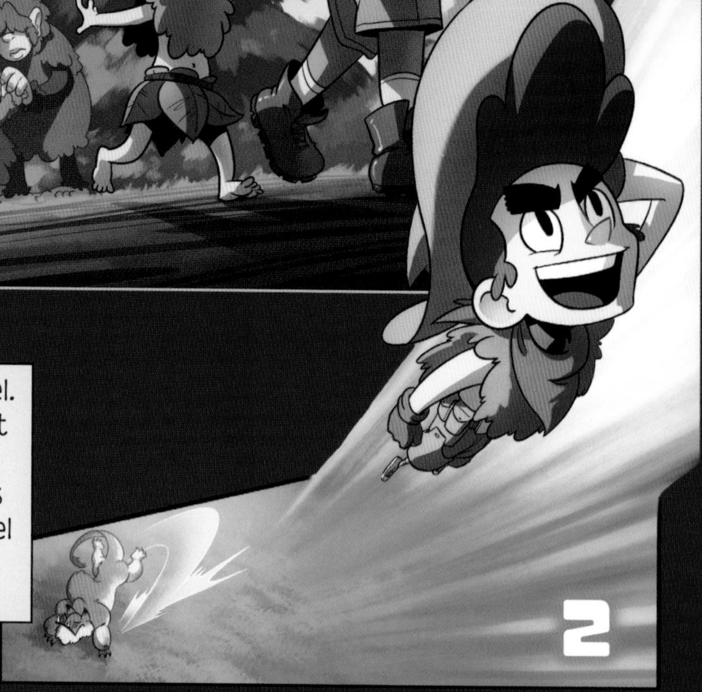
2

Bill is flying out of the panel. Why do you think the artist chose to draw the scene this way? What feeling does it create? How would it feel different if Bill was drawn inside the panel?

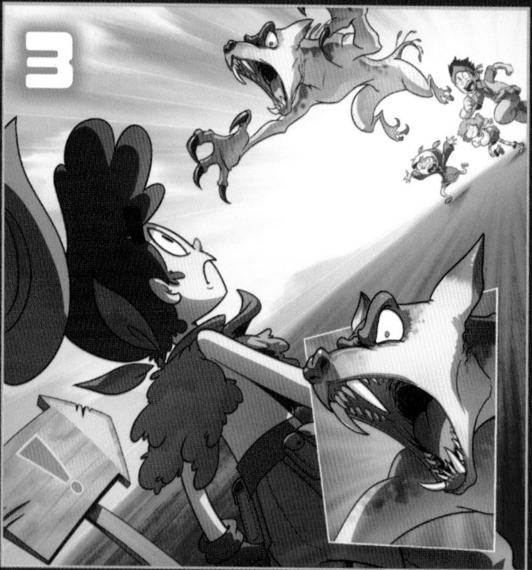
3

In comics, the end of a page is often used to create suspense. That's a term for when you're on the edge of your seat, wondering what will happen next. What were you expecting to happen after this panel on page 9? Were you surprised when you turned the page? Why or why not? Try finding other examples of a page turn leading to something unexpected.

In your own words, summarize how Bill saved the Crypto Ranch from the drought.

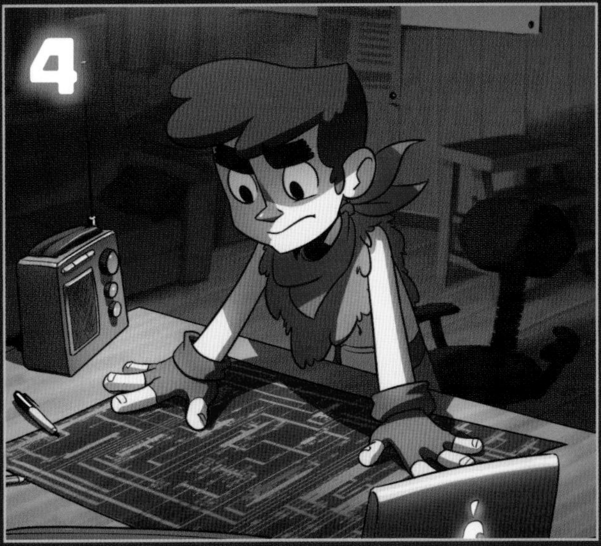
4

Do you think it was a good or bad idea for Sue to ride Petunia the bunyip? Write two paragraphs arguing for your answer, and be sure to back it up with examples from the story.

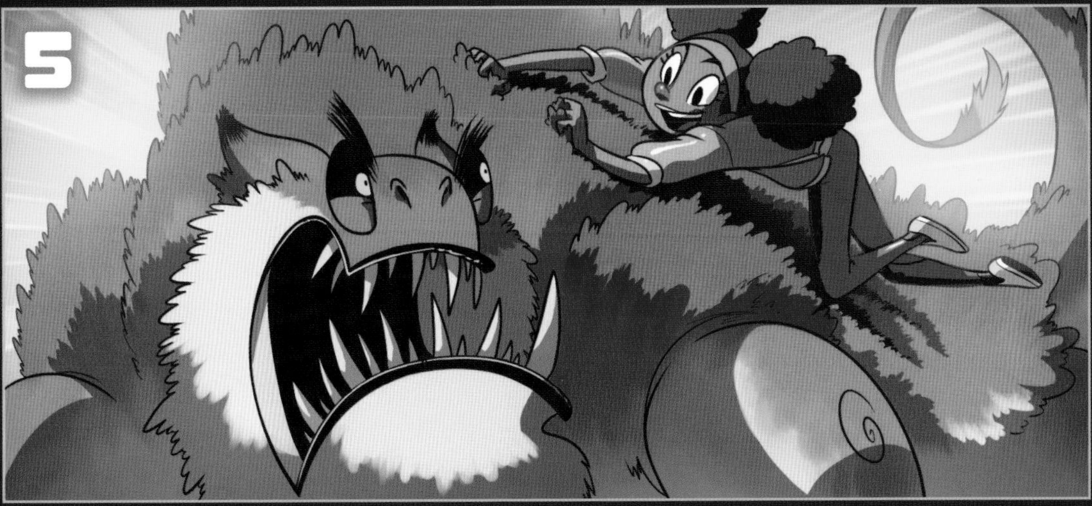
5

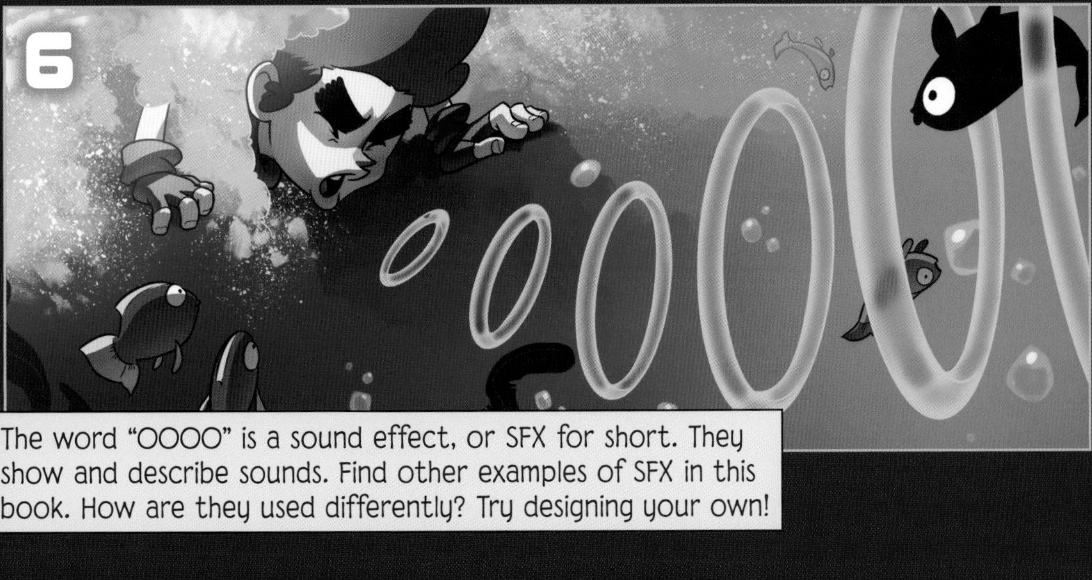
6

The word "OOOO" is a sound effect, or SFX for short. They show and describe sounds. Find other examples of SFX in this book. How are they used differently? Try designing your own!

AUTHOR

Benjamin Harper has worked as an editor at Lucasfilm LTD. and DC Comics. He currently lives in Los Angeles where he writes, watches monster movies, and hangs out with his cat Edith Bouvier Beale, III. His other books include the Bug Girl series, *Obsessed with Star Wars*, *Thank You, Superman!*, and *Hansel & Gretel & Zombies*.

ILLUSTRATOR

Fern Cano is an illustrator born in Mexico City, Mexico. He currently resides in Monterrey, Mexico, where he makes a living as an illustrator and colorist. He has done work for Marvel, DC Comics, and role-playing games like Pathfinder from Paizo Publishing. In his spare time, he enjoys hanging out with friends, singing, rowing, and drawing!

GLOSSARY

bunyip (BUHN-yip)—a monstrous animal said to live in Australia near watery areas; some legends say the creature eats people, but Pecos Bill knows how to make friends with one!

chupacabra (choop-ah-CAHB-rah)—a doglike creature said to live in North and South America that feeds on the blood of goats, sheep, and other animals

cryptid (KRIP-tid)—an animal whose existence has been suggested but never proven by scientists

drought (DROUT)—a long period of weather with little or no rain

expert (EK-spurt)—a person with a lot of knowledge in something

fabled (FAY-buhld)—told about in stories

ranch (RANCH)—a large farm for raising cattle, sheep, or horses (or legendary creatures!)

reservation (rez-er-VAY-shuhn)—a large area of land that is set aside for a special purpose (like protecting cryptids!)

Sasquatch (SAS-kwoch)—a hairy, ape-like creature said to live in the forests of the U.S. and Canada; also called Bigfoot

tabloid (TAB-loyd)—a newspaper that contains short stories and pictures meant to stir up interest or cause excitement

wrangle (RAYN-guhl)—to round up and care for animals

TRULY LEGENDARY TALES

FAR OUT FOLKTALES
BEST BOSS
JOHN HENRY, STEEL-DRIVIN' ELF
A GRAPHIC NOVEL
BY
BENJAMIN HARPER
ILLUSTRATED BY ALEX LOPEZ

FAR OUT FOLKTALES
JOHNNY SLIMESEED and the FREAKY FOREST
A GRAPHIC NOVEL
BY
STEPHANIE TRUE PETERS
ILLUSTRATED BY BERENICE MUNIZ

FAR OUT FOLKTALES
PAUL BUNYAN AND BABE THE BLUE WHALE
A GRAPHIC NOVEL
BY
PENELOPE GRUBER
ILLUSTRATED BY OTIS FRAMPTON

FAR OUT FOLKTALES
PECOS BILL, MONSTER WRANGLER
A GRAPHIC NOVEL

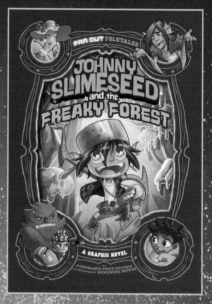

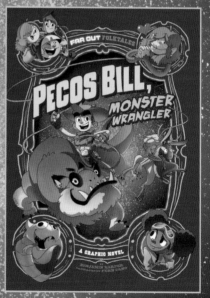

FAR OUT FOLKTALES

ONLY FROM capstone